GW00598852

THE FEVER OF THE

YEARS

e. b. baisden

Look at the land, the psalms
singing for our sons
beyond the fever of the years
and the clouds
The white precipitate of the sky
like incense on an altar

> *"Cane Garden"*
> *Daniel Williams*

THE FEVER OF THE YEARS
a collection of caribbean & american stories

e. b. baisden

Edited by
Grace Barrett

Preface by
Dr. J.A.G. Irish

Caribbean Research Center Press
Medgar Evers College, CUNY

Copyright (c) 1990 by E.B. Baisden
All Rights Reserved

Published by Caribbean Research Center Press
Medgar Evers College, CUNY
1150 Carroll Street
Brooklyn, NY 11225

Manufactured in the United States of America

First Edition

ISBN 1-878433-06-7

Dedicated to Grace Anne Barrett without whose constant
support this project would not have been completed,
to Carl Ballantyne, a keen critic and a great friend
and to J.A. George Irish, who continues to contribute to the
development of Caribbean scholarship and art

FOREWORD

This edition of short stories by E.B. Baisden comes as the second publication in the new literary thrust of the Creative Writers' Series of the Caribbean Research Center.

It follows the 1989 edition of <u>Native Landscapes : An Anthology of Caribbean Short Stories</u> which initiated the series.

The purpose of the series is to bring to light much of the new and hitherto hidden talent of promising unpublished young Caribbean writers with scarce opportunities to appear in print and who need a vehicle to guide and facilitate them.

Moreover, it is our intention to give expression to the experiences, dreams and visions of Caribbean peoples of the diaspora particularly here in the U.S.A. where very few of our writers have penetrated the market.

The Caribbean Research Center recognizes that this vibrant and diverse literary expression sustains and enriches the profound cultural connections between the Caribbean homelands and the adopted home of immigrant writers, and provides insights that social and economic analyses will never provide.

This is therefore a vital arm of the investigative and community outreach mission for which the Center was established. Its agenda must therefore go beyond demographics and statistical data, and explore the spiritual and cultural currents that sustain popular life.

J.A. George Irish

Contents

part I - love & despair

THE DAY THE CANOES CAME

It was Saturday afternoon, a quarter after one. Florence hadn't said anything for an hour. Her husband slept. She sat at the window and looked out at the harbor and the town. The island was obscure with a twilight that as of that day had lasted four hundred and ninety-four years.

"Even if electricity comes, it will still be twilight," Mannie said, slowly opening his eyes. He had said the same thing to her an hour ago and she had become silent and inscrutable. So he retreated to sleep in the rainbow colors of the hammock.

Now he was awakening, with his shirt unbuttoned and tiny beads of sweat blossoming like soft crystals among the hair on his chest. He wiped his face with his open palm, then rubbed at the sleep in his eyes with the back of his fists and saw Florence still sitting next to him on the stool at the window.

She turned slowly facing him. The small braids formed a dark semi-circle around her dark smooth face.

"You can say what you want. You play dominoes all day with your friends and look at the young girls and say, 'This year's crop is alright.'"

"But, my friends are all gone now," Mannie lamented, "gone to distant lands never to return."

Florence turned back to the window, folded her arms and rested her elbows and forearms on the windowsill, holding up the weight of the years of waiting. She had inherited this waiting from her mother, who had inherited it from her grandmother, who by then did not remember what she waited for and when she died, the men and women said, "She's gone to Guinea."

Neither could any of the women on St. Cortez remember why they sat and waited for hours at their windows, nor did they know whether the twilight would flower into day or darkness.

Five years ago the Prime Minister had said that the Americans were giving a generator to St. Cortez in exchange for his support in invading Grenada with frightened policemen. So, temporarily the women had something to wait for and after that they expected to sit and wait again.

"I dreamt last night of my dead grandmother and of many canoes in the bay filled with Black men. Their faces and chests were painted with purple and red."

Mannie sat up unsteadily in the hammock and began feeling for his sandals with his toes.

"You were dreaming with your stomach. It was digesting the burdens of your mind," Mannie said absently as his toes found the sandals. He bent forward, pulled the straps over the back of his heels and noticed how the wooden lengths of the floorboard were scrubbed into anonymity.

"I think the Americans will come today," Florence said. Mannie sighed, "The Americans can never reach Plower Island. Since Christopher Columbus, the island has measured time according to Queen Isabella's menstrual cycle. Each year we lose eleven days."

"You talk so much stupidness, stupidness."

"Serious, Florence. The generator is coming to us in the future and we are living in the past a hundred bloody periods behind."

Staring through the twilight at the dark bay, she ignored him.

"I'm going for a walk," he said, standing up and buttoning

his shirt. "I am going for a walk."

"To the bookstore, I bet?"

"To the bookstore."

"You are a sick man, Mannie."

Mannie stepped from the large wooden house that had been battered by time and heat into unsteady watercolors and shaky boards.

He relaxed in the circle of his head and walked his tall body downhill through the twilight along the stony path that led from the house. Surrounded by dark matted green shrubs, he looked down at the abscure town and could see a gathering of women along the shore. His eyes followed theirs over the dark waters of the bay where a muscular tug with a tall red and white chimney was pulling a barge. On it, a large rectangular object was hidden under an army-green tarpaulin.

"It looks like the generator has finally arrived," he thought as he stepped off the stony path onto the street and walked toward the bookstore past the two buildings of ulcered limestone and brown weathered shingles that stood on each side of the street at the entrance to Lordstown with its maze of narrow streets and the heavy perfume of trees that blossomed at night with dark purple flowers, and its antique two-story buildings of fading paint, strolling people, overhanging galleries, and broad-leafed breadfruit trees.

More women were walking toward the shore now, carrying plaited bamboo baskets of fruits on their heads and the old proprietor of the bookstore, black-bespectacled and bald-pated, with suspenders and khaki shirt, stood under the arches in the doorway with his hands in his pockets. He spoke as Mannie approached.

"Look like we will soon have electricity and the children will stop reading."

"It will still be twilight and all day Lordstown will look like blurred pictures of New York City at night," Mannie replied.

The proprietor nodded and stepped aside. Mannie walked into the bookstore among the long dim corridors of shelves, flickering lamplight and silently aging books closed on the mystery of the worlds inside them.

He walked to the back of the dim corridor to the green door closed to the curious school children, turned its brass handle below the sign with the word 'Private' and walked to a glass case filled with imported pictures of naked bodies and faces, intent and focused toward harsh silent gasps. His eyes roamed toward the black and white and green cover of a magazine with a picture of a fat, dark Brazilian transvestite with breasts and a huge penis and a very pale woman sitting next to him on a white sheeted bed. The green tint of the picture made her paleness seem immoral and made the transvestite surreal shrouded in green against the white sheet.

Mannie could hear the chatter of the waiting women outside on the shore. He recalled the tale of his grandmother. A tale of African women newly brought to the islands who gathered on the beach and built a fire so that when they jumped over it they would be transported to Africa.

He thought of his wife sitting in the window waiting and knew she was ashamed of the loud and common lot waiting for the Americans on the shore. She had class and the distance that came from a long line of school teachers and nurses and haughty unsmiling mothers.

The proprietor came in and Mannie paid him for the magazine. He could not let Florence see it. He turned, lifted his shirt and hid it. His belt held it firm, flat and disguised against his stomach. Then he stepped out of the bookstore and walked along Early Street to the shore among the gathering of expectant women dressed in white, with white cloth tied above their smooth black faces, chatting with smiling white teeth and pious with red and white parrots on their shoulders.

They had covered the coral beach with their dark ankles

and well-rounded calves below the sour tamarind rolled in sugar and a colorful array of fruits, carved birds and mahagony men playing steel drums in painted straw hats glistening with new varnish. Oranges, yucca, bananas, mangoes, and green avacadoes glittered just beyond the silent white surf.

Mannie followed their excited, pious eyes out to sea. There steaming toward the shore behind the bulldog tug and the generator were two grey battleships, and as soon as they entered the harbor, sailors filled the rowboats on the decks and were lowered onto the dark waters with rope and pulleys. When the boats touched the waters and the rope was cast off, the sailors rowed hurriedly to the shore and jumped from the boats wetting their polished black shoes and white bell-bottomed pants in the surf and they mingled among the women, their hands filled with strips of glowing metal that looked like new spanners which had had their useful ends removed. The sailors ignored the fruit and the carved musicians and moved hurriedly among the women offering the strips of metal and passages on the battleships to America.

Mannie looked around him amazed at the mobile scene of twilight filled with sparkling teeth of giggling women bargaining with the men, and then he saw his wife among the women.

She didn't see him and was trying to slip a strip of metal from a table into her pocket before the sailor who owned them saw her. She looked up and saw Mannie looking at her. He shrugged. The sailor, blond and white, looked around, saw her, winked and smiled. Jealousy and despair filled Mannie. Florence remained expressionless.

The thought of Florence and another man made him jealous and he was confused by the pleasure thickening in his crotch. The sailor walked over to Florence, putting his arm around her. She looked at Mannie. He shrugged again and felt the smoothness of the magazine against his stomach. Florence shook the sailor's arm from her shoulder and vanished in the crowd.

Mannie searched for her, walking through the crowd on the beach and stepping over sailors grunting between dark legs above the holes that crabs had made deep in the sand, and the fruits and the carved mahogany musicians scattered on the beach and rolling in the surf.

He searched for his wife, ashamed, lonely, lamenting for his friends who had left and gone to distant lands. He walked toward the seashore in the murky half night that according to legend was first seen by the dying stare of Indians run through by swords blessed with holy water and further darkened by the longing of Africans to return home.

As he walked along the seashore he saw Florence. She was sitting in a rowboat on the dark water naked beneath a shiny, tight saffron nightgown. There were other women sitting in the boat with her, waiting for the sailors to row them to the ships.

She looked at him and her eyes said that she hoped he didn't mind, but she was tired of waiting and so she was leaving for another land.

The sailors pushed out the oars splashing the water, awakening the sleeping crayfish and the souls of the dead waiting in the water to be reborn.

Then they began rowing the boat out toward the ships in the twilight bay.

TELL IT TO MY DOG

'Gents Shoe Store, Lordstown, St. Cortez ... '. Sapitz the watchman, took off his thick glasses, cleaned the lens on the chest of his soiled white shirt and recognized again the letters on the large cardboard carton in the ship's cargo bay.

He shook his head, hooked his thumbs into his worn red suspenders, and looked at the stevedores loading the cargo onto the lift with sullen impatience. In the enclosed silence of his head, he shouted at them. "Leave. Go to lunch. This minute. Right now." He stretched the elastic suspenders away from his chest and looked down. Below the cuffed ankles of his stained khaki pants, the oxfords he wore were disfigured, scruffed and almost flat to the ground. 'And every damn oxford in that box is new,' he thought and began to pace back and forth. His eyes focused on the cardboard carton. His own shoes were a used gift from his boss, the old Englishman, Mr. Guinness.

Sapitz had a weakness for oxfords and the assumptions he connected to them. When asked his occupation, he replied, "A gentleman, a scholar .... and a distant cousin to the Queen." He wept when England lost at cricket or soccer and his lifetime goal was to read the works of "that ole chap, what's his name, ah yes, William." Recently he had included in his ambitions the memorization of 'King Lear'.

One day Mr. Guinness told him, "Sapitz, you simply cannot read the book that way. It is turned upside down."

At twelve noon the stevedores left the cargo bay. When the last man had climbed the ladder welded to the side of the cargo bay Sapitz peered all around him through the transparent spirals in his thick glasses. Satisfied that no-one was around he ripped the carton with the square, muscular force of his big hands, and took out a shiny, brand spanking new pair of oxfords, the biggest in the box, with tassels and fake holes.

Hiding behind a wooden crate he held the shoes close to his face and spit all over them. Then with his knife he stabbed a bag of cement, took out a handful and dusted it on the new shoes. The spit held the cement to the leather, making the shoes appear dirty and used. Then bending over, he took off his old oxfords, put on the new pair, straightened up, looked down at the new shoes and stomped twice. The cement held but the new shoes were tight on his feet below his baggy, banana stained khaki pants.

He smiled, satisfied. His eyes danced, small, dizzy, jittery black beans behind the spinning spirals in the lens of his glasses. Now he truly felt truly like an Oxford don, a gentlemen, a scholar, a distant cousin to the Queen.

The stevedores came back from lunch at one o'clock. By then his feet were burning in the shoes. To silence the pain he began to limp slightly. The stevedores noticed the change of shoes and smiled.

All went well. The stevedores went home, the ship sailed from Lordstown harbor, and Sapitz went back on guard in the empty, fenced banana compound.

At five, Mr Guiness drove his white Jaguar to the gates.

He saw Sapitz cussing mad and pelting his dog Julie with stones.

"You damn greedy backside slut. You nasty bitch."

The dog ran to the gate and began to squeeze under the tall gate of steel mesh. A stone hit the dog's leg. Julie yelped and Mr. Guiness stepped on the brake.

Sapitz turned, saw Mr. Guiness, bowed, took a quick glance at his new oxfords, bowed again and said, "Nice day sir. Good afternoon sir."

Julie squeezed under the gate and ran off howling.

Sapitz pushed open the gates. Mr. Guinness lit a cigarette and waited. Through the smoke he noted that Sapitz limped, then he drove off and Sapitz ran alongside the car bowing, limping and scraping and wishing him, "Good afternoon and have a nice sleep sir, yes sir ..."

"New oxfords, but of course."

Mr. Guiness pushed on the brakes. The car stopped. Sapitz, still running and limping, came to a stop in front of the car. He turned out of breath and saw Mr. Guiness peering over the dash board, looking at his new shoes. Sapitz saluted him. Mr Guinness put away his cigarette and removed his spectacles. Quickly Sapitz began to limp back into the compound. Over his shoulder he saw Mr. Guinness cleaning his spectacles. Sapitz hurried. Mr. Guinness put on his spectacles, turned and aimed his stare at the feet of the rapidly departing Sapitz.

"Sapitz."

"Yes Sir."

Sapitz looked back at Mr. Guinness. Through the tunnels of the transparent spirals of their glasses their beady eyes met and Sapitz stood alone in his oxfords in the wide empty compound. He tugged at his suspenders, followed Mr. Guinness' eyes downwards at the dusty cement caked oxfords and awaited the pronouncement of his fate from the man who sometimes drove back to the compound late at night to marvel at the length and thickness of his banana.

Sapitz didn't think of his years of service, his waiting and watching in the banana compound which was busy on day a week when the trucks brought bananas from the countryside estates where the peasants planted the banana tree and the YessirSirs owned and sold the green fruit. That day the women milled about like ants in the banana compound working, dressed in cheap print, balancing bunches of green banana on steady heads with their backs straight, their behinds cocked back, hurrying from truck to conveyor belts loading bananas into the black holes of white ships tied to the docks in the deep blue seawater of Lordstown harbor.

Looking at the old English man, what Sapitz did think about was Miss Princess with her six children none of them his but all have different fathers. If Mr. Guinness fired him. Oh Jesus Christ! What would Miss Princess say? For every day of the fifteen years that he worked at the compound he thought of Miss Princess. On Wednesdays he worked double. He was watchman and stevedore unloading cloth and shoes and baby powder and bolts and radios and whatsnot made in England, America and Japan for the stores of the bill of laden capitalists of St. Cortez. His dog Julie, a white mongrel, part daschund with a black patch over her left eye, worked double too, watching with one eye open and sleeping on her long stomach with her wet nose and long face stretched out along the length of the wharf alongside the white length of the ship.

Sometimes Sapitz went to mow and trim Mr. Guinness' hedge but most of the time he stayed and watched in the banana compound, day and night with his dog Julie, a damn good dog and he had two damn good hens that woke Sapitz with barking and cackling if someone tried to enter the compound.

For years Sapitz watched a woman called Miss Princess from behind the fence of the compound. He saw her belly swell up and go down four times making it 2, 3, 4, 5, ... 6 children - two boys and four girls, none look like the other but he was still afraid to talk to Miss Princess.

It wasn't until one night when Mr. John, the shipping supervisor brought her to the banana shed, that Sapitz pumped up enough courage to ask her.

"Could you marry me Miss Princess? Is long time well I wanted to ask you but ..." She didn't cuss him. She only buttoned her blouse and took a good look at him up and down from head to toe and toe to head. From that night Sapitz started sending her money and gifts. One clear night when the sky was filled up with shooting stars, she came to visit him at the compound and called him her gentleman friend.

A month later Mr. Redman made his suit and Miss Princess married Sapitz. He only went home one day a month. The day when he got his pay. If the moon wasn't bleeding, they went in the bedroom and he put his hand in his pocket and gave her all the money. She gave him a few dollars back and warned him not to spend it all for she might need something during the month, and afterwards he sat at the table and ate some food and watched the children, proud that the two older boys were going to secondary school. The two boys would look back at him, disgusted that he was there with his old baggy pants and his sour felt hat.

In August, a month before Hurricane Melda, one of his fowls began to lay eggs and it made him worry a little and scratch his head and smell the sweat under his cap because one morning Mr. Guinness, after he had parked his car and was walking toward the office, saw Sapitz throwing corn on the ground for the three fowls he kept there. Mr. Guinness walked past him and two minutes later, Mr. John, the shipping supervisor came down from the office.

"Sapitz, you not allowed to bring more than two fowls on the compound."

So two weeks after, when the hen started sitting he took eleven of the dozen eggs from under the hen, she pecked him, and he sent the eggs for Miss Princess.

The next Wednesday, he got four large white round eggs from the fat English cook in the galley of the ship.

When he told the fat cook that he was going to hatch them, the cook laughed, pushed up his white sleeve over white arms and told him in cockney that the eggs couldn't hatch because they weren't cocked, but he didn't believe the fat white cook, for 'that is such stupidness, what hen could lay eggs without being cocked?' That afternoon he pushed them under the still setting hen, imagining the big white English chickens that should soon be hatching. The setting hen ruffled her feathers and pecked him four times.

But Goddammit man, six nights later - the night before he stole the oxfords - while he was sleeping, the damn dog Julie chased the hen from off the nest. He remembered hearing the hen cackle but Sapitz didn't get up, and Julie sucked every damn egg.

That morning Sapitz beat the dog so bad that it howled for the devil and the angels all at the same time and squeezed under the fence of the compound with Sapitz holding his glasses with one hand and throwing licks on its behind with a piece of wood in the other. But Julie had come back that afternoon wagging "her damn slut backside tail" and he pelt stones at her and sent her off hopping and howling and squeezing under the gate. That was when Mr. Guinness drove up.

And there he stood looking up from the new cement oxfords with Mr Guinness looking at him and Sapitz knew that his fate would be decided in terms of the great name of Oxford.

But Mr. Guinness did not say anything to Sapitz. He drove off and Sapitz suspected why. He breathed out a long sigh and sat down flat on the ground, looked up to heaven and said, "Thank you God. You hear. Thank the good living God, thanks."

He got up, closed the gates, walked into the compound and found Mr. John, the boasting shipping supervisor waiting on him.

"Sapitz you're fired."

"Who say that?"

"Mr. Guinness phoned."

Sapitz walked slowly home to Miss Princess. He hadn't gone home for about a year since the night he had ague and fever and went home because the banana compound was near the sea and the shed was drafty, and he met a gentleman caller of the house, a young inspector of police who walked as though he wanted to push his chest to the other side of the street, there with Miss Princess, and Sapitz bawled out, "Oh Jesus Christ, ah weh the ass me seeing here." Then he tried to put blows on the Miss Princess, but she reach for the high heel shoe under the bed and he kicked her in the belly and the inspector watched and yes, she knocked off her husband glasses and when Sapitz was crawling 'bout under the bed looking for the glasses, and she beat him some more and the inspector pull her away, and Sapitz heard the bed begin to creak again while he was crawling 'round blind, like Bartimeus feeling for the glasses and when he found 'the damn stupid glasses' and put them on he took another look to make sure, and he shouted again "Oh Jesus Christ ah dead you hear" and he ran out of the house.

So from that day, he never went back home but lived all week, seven days, twenty four seven, within the circle of watching, seeing the sun rise and fall from inside the banana compound with his dog Julie and the two hens.

And Miss Princess tall son, the one that was Lawyer Woodley's child, well he came to the compound every Wednesday to get the money for his mother and Sapitz would send home every cent for Miss Princess and the boy would bring back a few dollars for him.

So now after he was fired he was thinking as he walked up Halifax Street, 'She shouldn't mind if I come home now.'

When Sapitz reached home Miss Princess was happy to see him. He didn't say anything, and she threw her arms around him and he took off his hat and he held his head down. Then Sapitz went into the bathroom and it felt better than hanging his naked backside over the sea on the docks at night and hearing it drop plop in the water. When he came out of the bathroom she had some food for him, so he sat at the table holding the knife and fork upright as he chewed and looked around him, admiring the children and how they grew. When he finished eating she sent him off to work. That was when he told her he had no work and she took off her shoe and beat him all the way down Halifax Street.

He had nowhere to go so he walked back to the banana compound and found the gates locked and met his dog Julie waiting outside the gates and Julie looked up at him with big friendly eyes and wagged her tail.

The new watchman, who was a stevedore that Sapitz knew, came to the gate and told him to pitch his tail away from there, so that night he slept under Gents Shoe Store gallery with his dog Julie, on a broad piece of cardboard with his two fowls next to him in a box, and he was sleeping there a week later when the hurricane came.

Two months later because the new watchman was a much bigger thief than Sapitz and for other reasons Mr. Guinness gave Sapitz back his job and Julie and the two fowls went back to work too, barking and cackling every night.

Sapitz still there, still watching in the banana compound, wearing the glasses with spiraling circles and the baggy khaki pants and his oxfords with fake holes. He still does send home the pay to Miss Princess but lately there was one change in the routine of his life, he developed the curious habit of eating out of the same bowl with his dog Julie.

THE LIBERATION OF
MISS PRINCESS

When Princess first came to Lordstown she had wanted to
be a carpenter for she was ambitious and only had less than a
primary school education, so instead of wanting to be a
servant girl in somebody's big house she wanted a skill and
came to Lordstown from the country side one carnival Tuesday
and slept by Ma Patsy on some old cloth on the pitch pine floor
for Ma Patsy was she mother's friend and lived in Flower
Garden in a one room with her coal pot outside in the dirt yard
in front the door, where Ma Patsy used to cook for the four
children them, one child grown up and left, but still coming
back looking for food,and the other three knocking 'bout the
place.

On Ash Wednesday morning Ma Patsy wake up Miss
Princess and ask her what she want to do in Lordstown and
she told her a mechanic work, so Ma Patsy walked with her to

Old Jonas carpenter shop and asked him to take her on. The sad thin faced shop-owner smiled and said, "Girl if you can find one woman carpenter in all of St. Cortez I will take you on as an apprentice."

So Princess searched around and asked around and there was no woman carpenter on St. Cortez. She went back to Mr. Jonas and told him and he said, "That's what I tell you girl, tradition, I can't take you on."

She didn't understand his reasoning but decided that she would be a car mechanic instead and went to Mr. Langley garage to see if he would take her on.

She talked to the bald head, bony mechanic in Mr. Langley yard who was filing down the filler on an old bang up Chevy raised up on a jack in the hot sun under a big mango tree. He didn't answer her, instead he called out laughing.

"Eh Spence, listen to this nuh." A dirty man with tough grease in his clothes pushed himself out from under the old Chevy. He listened to Princess, and laughed too, then stared at her up and down like if she put on her dress on the wrong side that morning and he said , "Well is what the ass me hearing here. You sure she ain't crazy."

"Spence, call Mr. Langley for she."

Spence went into the two storey wooden house and Mr.

Langley came downstairs tall black and shine, grinning gold teeth, and he said to her, "Yes, well come upstairs and I will teach you."

So she went upstairs and became one of his women and make a child for him. He rented a room for her in Flower Gardens next to Ma Patsy and put her in it, but soon he didn't want to give her money to support the child and so she started learning how to turn her hand like the other poor good looking women in Flower Garden who also had child and children but no job and no steady man. Soon she was collecting pum pum gratuity.

One day when she was walking uptown she looked over her shoulder and saw Lawyer Woodley parked in his car on Halifax Street eyeing her from behind, she was looking good, pretty with cat eyes and red hair, young and from the back her future was looking bright in the tight jeans pants, so she eyed him back and smiled at him over her shoulder and walked away stepping nice and curving her waist. He drove up alongside her and after that he started visiting her late at night and paying the rent and giving her money to buy milk for the child. She made the second child for he.

All this time well she mastering 'turning she hand' so she had a fisherman who give her fish early in the morning when the seine come in and she cooked for the children, a shopkeeper who gave her rice and butter, a police inspector, a lawyer and two merchants who gave her status and always could give her a car ride and dollars that she could buy other things with to smell nice and look good, and when she got pregnant she would always say the belly is for one of the big men and it must be true for one of the boys red and tall just like the Lawyer Woodley and the other one short and bragging like Inspector Hill. One day John, the seine-captain asked her when she goin' to make belly for he and she kiss up her teeth and walk off.

And by the night the fool fool watchman named Sapitz asked her to marry him she had rented a house, taken on boarders and lodgers, and had little embarrassments, for she was looking good and considered herself to be fully middle class for she had children for lawyer, doctor and police inspector and she knew how to put her hand on her hip, lift up her head high with a sneer on her face just like the Governor General wife to show she was superior to anyone who felt otherwise. To crown that she claimed family to once prominent dead lawyer and had some respect for she wouldn't answer for nothing if she wasn't called Miss Princess. After a while she wouldn't even piss on the fisherman and shopkeepers them for she had just enough money to buy fish and butter and rice but the children were getting older and she wanted to send them to a secondary school.

She married Sapitz the watchman, for whatever reasons. Some people say because he spent all the time, day and night in the banana compound.

The night when he lost his job she beat him and chase him out, Sapitz went and talked to Ma Patsy, and Ma Patsy asked Miss Princess why she treat the man like that she said, "Well, heh, somebody got to pay."

THE BALL

That Thursday morning, like every morning, Carlos jogged up Zion Hill. He was tall, good-looking, wore flag-red shorts and as he ran up toward the hilltop it rushed away from him. He chased it, hard sweat in his eyes, his breath clouding his glasses. "C'mon, you can do it," he thought. "Shorter strides. More push. When will all these problems be over." He ran. "C'mon, more push and when all these problems are over, how will they have been resolved? Push. Push. C'mon, now." In a burst of speed he ran at the summit; it rushed away from him. Abruptly in mid-stride he gave up and sat down on the grass at the side of the road sucking in and blowing out sudden pockets of air. His body heaved. His bearded face hung forward toward his knees.

There was sweat on his arms and legs . He felt himself becoming distorted, huge, self-absorbed, trying to catch up with the exhaustion of his breathing and the effort of living in the hot, sunny, soundless morning.

Behind and above him, a yellow tennis ball began to roll downhill.

He had been fired. Mr. Ledlow fired him with a wife and two children and petit-bourgeois status. Now he couldn't even afford a drink of rum. In the corner of his vision, the quick yellow edge of a blur. He turned. His hard eyes focused on the luminous yellow tennis ball rolling downhill on the black street.

On impulse he got up and ran after it. He imagined a boy would soon come running, looking for the ball. Carlos chased the ball. He didn't want to catch it. He wanted to see how far it would roll before something or someone stopped it. Then he would pick it up and throw it to the boy.

He ran in jerks, breaking the downward speed of the hill with long muscular legs. His jerking rhythm lurched the blue-green water of the harbor and the town far below him.

He could see the red tops of the houses of Lordstown, far below; its labyrinth of streets, the white ship and the ceaseless toil of miniature workers loading it with bananas.

He had come back home St. Cortez after studying anthropology in New York City. Five other graduates returned to St. Cortez around the same time he did. They were all from established families, arrogant with their University degrees, critical and brimming with radical solutions to the plight of St. Cortez. They asked him to speak with them at a public meeting in the town square.

He had been ambivalent about speaking out. He had admitted to himself that he had no social conscience. He was now a socially accepted part of the secret society of the middle-class. But he knew that these fellows were the future big boys and he wanted to be in their company. That heady night with its crowd of cheering young men and tall policemen standing in the background, looking uncomfortable in their black tunics and the old poor who had brought their boxes and stools to sit up front listening with hopeful attentive adoring eyes, that night he got ahead of himself and made the mistake of referring to the Minister of Education in analogy over a loudspeaker in the Town Square at the crowded public meeting.

In small, hot countries, political power is like the bad breath of a friend.

"The educational system," he had said, "reflects the

country's underdevelopment and produces bloated arrogant men expert at flawed Latin phrases, like the Education Minister, Mr. Ledlow."

He had said it out of spite and because it was true and because the Minister's wife had invited his wife and himself to tea at her house and the Minister had purposefully ignored him.

The next day he had regretted saying it, for Mr. Ledlow, a bald, bow-legged and bespectacled man who had never left the island and had been secure till then within the gravity of his personality, despite his asthma, despite what the Syrian cloth merchant was doing with his wife, despite all -- his flawed Latin made him muscular, guttural, and unforsaken like a Socialist behind a beard, like a Christian in front of a cross.

And so with a certainty of self beyond faith, Mr. Ledlow drove his creaking black Morris Oxford uphill toward Lordstown Grammar School between two lines of palm trees, with his jaws clenched, the wrinkles on his brown face, sinewy and sculptured like muscles. He braked in front of the white four-story building, slammed the car door, rushed up the stairs, and burst into Carlos' classroom slamming the door against the wall. Carlos was standing there, his back to the door. He jumped, ducked, turned, and saw the Minister rushing toward him. A cloud of chalkdust lifted from the blackboard. Carlos stepped back. Then he stood his ground. The well-trained khaki-clad pupils in Upper Three became quietly excited.

The Minister put his fist under Carlos' nose, menacing him, embarrassing him in front of the boys who would in turn tell their parents.

"Do you smell this?"

Carlos could smell the fist. It had no particular smell. The Minister's face was huge and close. Their glasses were almost touching. Carlos counted five giant grey hairs in Ledlow's left eyebrow. Carlos' blood boiled but he didn't want to lose his job.

He was stepping away from Ledlow when a knuckle rubbed the tip of his nose.

Automatically, Carlos grabbed the Minister's fist and the students went wild, rushing over desks, surrounding the two grown men. Carlos held the Minister's arm by the wrist and began to push it back to where he felt "it damned well belonged" at the Minister's side. The Minister pushed back. Furious. He had never met a man yet he didn't feel superior to and who was this upstart, son of a damn blasted market women. A battle of strength and will began.

The noisy boys were frantic, joyously divided in their support. "C'mon Teach," they screamed. Two boys began to chase three others knocking over desks in a maddening clatter. A rowdy circle of boys shouted, "C'mon Ledlow."

"I betcha Teach win,"

"I bet ya not."

"C'mon Teach." A shout from the back.

"C'mon Mr. Ledlow. Move yo' backside man." The boys laughed. The Minister's anger flared. His face puffed and bulged. The veins in his neck sweated. He was determined to push his fist right into Carols' nose. Carlos was quietly strong.

The yellow ball began picking up speed. Carlos ran more freely downhill. The ball appeared fluorescent and blurred against the black street. Carlos ran after it.

Against Carlos' silent strength, the Minister's arm had weakened. Then Carlos began pushing it down to his side. The Minister pushed back. The boys became quiet and tense. For some reason, the boys didn't understand when it was obvious that their teacher was winning, he released his downward force on the Minister's wrist. Ledlow's fist rose rapidly. Carlos tried to step back. The fist connected. Carlos' glasses flew up from his nose, then down. The blood burst and splattered on his white shirt. He stepped back, removed his glasses, held his head down and was reaching in his pocket for a handkerchief when he heard.

"You're fired. Go work with your mother in the market."

Carlos looked up and saw the Minister walking from the room. He went after him and brought him back by the collar, with a fist to his ear.

Now, he ran downhill after the ball.

The Teacher's Union objected to the firing, saying that actually the Minister had gone up to the school looking for trouble and it was he who first assaulted Carlos. So, filled with moral might and the right to vote, the union went on strike. On small hot Caribbean islands, issues of principle are interpreted personally. Ten more teachers were fired before the strike ended. The Union took the matter to court where the Minister's son was the Attorney General.

Carlos had expected the ball to stop rolling by now, to have rushed off the street and into the grass. It hadn't.

He hadn't wanted to get married either. He had come back home on summer vacation and Wilhelmina felt good pressed against the downstairs of her father's house.

"Don't even think about her," he said to himself, chasing the ball.

And, every morning, there was a pain in the back of his head. "It must be a tumor," he thought.

"Was it a tumor?"

"Don't even think about that."

But the worried thoughts filled his head, screaming and pushing at the closed circle of his skull. He was becoming dizzy and unfocussed.

The speeding ball became a rushing blur of blue phospherescence. The street glowed shiny and black. His worrries pushed themselves at him. Would he get his job back? He pushed back at the thoughts, focussing on the speed of the ball. It was rushing off the street. Now it was at the turn of the corner. He ran after it.

When he was a boy, he played a game with a penny. Toss it in the air, ask a question, if the coin landed on heads, the answer was yes. If it landed on tails, the answer was no. He decided to play a similar game with the ball.

He said to himself. "If the ball makes it around the corner, I will get my job back. If it doesn't, well ..."

He ran after the ball. The ball neared the downhill curve, it picked up speed. It began to swerve off the road.

His heartbeat quickened. He was dizzy. His head was spinning in the heat. That's it for the job then. An empty nausea, light and sickly, filled his stomach. The world filled him and his head and the sweat on his legs. The ball, flecked with fluorescense on the black street and the green grass. A car rushed uphill. He swerved out of its path. The ball hit the tire of the car. It bounced back toward the street, rolled around the corner and continued rolling. Carlos breathed out heavily. The ball became yellow again, ordinary. He ran and picked it up.

"Mister, can I have my ball?"

He turned. A small, skinny girl with her hand outstretched wearing blue pants, torn at the knees, and a red plaid shirt with missing buttons, looked up at him with a quizzical smile on her face.

He smiled, looked at the ball, then looked back at her. He had plans for the ball. It had become his oracle. He would roll it downhill and know the outcome of whatever he asked it, for better or worse. He would know and adjust to the future no matter how dire.

"I'll give you your ball. But just let me roll it again a few times." The little girl cocked her head to one side, rolled her eyes and put her hand on her hip.

"Ah, c'mon." He smiled and pinched her cheek.

After a long moment, she said, "All right."

He now wanted to ask about his wife. Would his marriage last? Recently Wilhelmina's face had taken on a distant snobbish defen-siveness. A look that Cortezians used together with quotes from Shakespeare and sentences in flawed Latin to buttress illusions of their distinction.

The hardship of living had settled over her. She no longer had the gaiety with which women deluded men into committing themselves. That had fooled him into thinking that she would be whatever he wanted her to be.

She had done a lot of living since their first child was born in New York in his final year at the University. They had loud arguments and fist fights with bites and scratches. He had to pay school fees and buy books and go to school and study and work. But after the third month of her pregnancy, when her body had become accustomed to the unbalance of hormones, she stopped fighting and her stomach grew bigger. He remained rude and withdrawn and he hated her.

That was when the gaiety began to leave her and the defiance disfigured her face. This was all his mother's fault. For who were the Murray's anyway.

Now again, since he wasn't working, she had slowly began acting her part in the marriage from an increasing distance. She had been encouraging at first, then hesitant, and now she hardly smiled in his presence. She had never before asked him about the white woman. "With that sour smell of ice", she said. "Yes, the peace corps volunteer you have." Now she asked him about Helen at night when he reached for her, and before she pushed him away.

"Mister," the little girl said impatiently.

He looked down at her large, silent eyes, and at the ball in his hand. The street stretched out before him. About twenty yards away next to the street was pink house with a red roof. The girl put both hands on her hips and began tapping her foot. He decided to roll the ball. If it rolled into the gutter before it passed the house, then it meant that the marriage would not last.

"O.K. One minute," he said to the little girl. "I want to roll it again." He rested the ball on the street and with his forefinger he pushed it forward. It rolled downhill. He ran after the ball and the girl ran after him.

He had loved Wilhelmina the summer he came home on vacation. In September, he flew back to New York, and had settled into the fall semester. When his mother wrote to him:

"Dear Carlos,

So you bring scandal on the people. You gone and make Mr. Murray girl child pregnant. Well, I telling you now. You got to marry her. I talk to the father last night. Is true when I let out my rooster I ain't call no fowl. But I agree with him and she mother was crying. Poor woman. He say he posting she for you and I agree with him. Yes, yes and you better marry her.

You hear me Carlos ..."

The next day he got a letter from Wilhelmina. She told him about the pregnancy and that her father had booked her a flight arriving at JFK on November 15.

The ball was picking up speed. The girl chased him He ran faster. He ran close to the ball, his sneakers hitting the street next to it. Almost immediately it rolled from the middle of the road swerving left and toward the gutter.

" ... and damn my mother anyway and damn all these stupid people on this two-by-four island and the preposterous reality they have set up. For if it was Maud daughter I'd left with the belly, I'd bet she would not have said a damn thing. She would have said I let out me rooster I ain't call no roach and that would be that. She would not have written. I know her. But the Murrays, no, they are the big bowties. All the time the father was embezzling the blasted bank money."

After the baby was born, Wilhelmina got a job and moved out of his Brooklyn apartment. They saw each other off and on. She regrouped her mystique of a well-mannered snob and he fell in love with her again.

When he received the diploma that read "Bachelor of Arts" he went back to St. Cortez without her.

His mother's wooden house embarrassed him and it embarrassed him that she was a market vendor with a loud mouth and a sharp tongue who tied her head with bright print cloth. If he had to go to the Lordstown market for any reason, he ignored her. She was always chatting commess with the other women. He would not see her nor say hello to her. Sometimes he would see her finger pointing and he knew she was telling one of them women, "That's me son."

One of his new friends, a PhD, Oxford said to him one day, "Look. St. Cortez is a small pool and small fishes are bigger here. In London and New York, well, let's be honest, we are just faces in the crowd." Carlos, with his degree went up in social rank and he settled at once into the illusions of St. Cortez social ranking. He wrote to Wilhelmina and asked her to come home with his child. On St. Cortez she had social status. When Wilhelmina came home, he married her.

The ball was rolling now at the edge of the street. It was about ten yards from the pink house. He doubted it would pass the house without rolling into the gutter. He hated the damn ball. It threatened him. It threatened the life he had become accustomed to. He could not imagine leaving his kids. He ran close to it bringing down his foot hard on its left side trying to shake it back onto the road away from the gutter. It now appeared brown as through it was made of iron with sharp spikes torturing him and threatened to deny what he had struggled so hard for. "Anyway," he thought. "I can always marry Helen..... if I do the guys would snob me."

On St. Cortez, white women were no longer in vogue.
The ball rolled speedily downhill. Now it was on the edge of the street. The pink house seemed far away. The little girl ran after him. His feet thundered behind the ball. He thought of his mother. He felt himself sagging inside. His muscular legs were becoming soft. It pained him to go to his mother's house to get food so that he could feed his wife and two children. It pained him more when he had to go to the market and be seen loading the bolts of cloth and provisions into his car and to have her introduce him as "This is me big son, Carlos. The one who wins the scholarship to the University." Then he had to drive her home, for she had told him. "Carlos if you can't help, boy you can't eat from me labor."

Jogging downhill now was infinitely more difficult. He chased the ball and watched it as it left the edge of the street - five feet or so from the pink house and rolled into the gutter.

He ran, bent over and picked it up. It was hard and hot in his hand. He squeezed it as hard as he could but it didn't burst. He wanted it to burst 'goddammit'. He slammed it on the street. It bounced high in the air and the little girl ran past him, stood under it. The ball hung for a moment in the air. The girl stared up at it, cupped her two hands. It fell in line with her face, she caught it, and turned to where he stood with his head bent. "Do you hate my ball? Do you want to burst it?"

"No," he said looking at her, sad, dejected. "Could I roll it again? One more time?"

"No," she said walking away uphill, taking the ball with her. "I think the ball make you sad. He walked after her. "Maybe, but, just once more," he pleaded. She continued walking. He looked at the back of her small body in the red-plaid shirt walking away from him. Then she turned and brought the ball to him.

"O.K. Just one more time."

He took the ball. Carlos was now about halfway downhill about five hundred yards from Lordstown. A reinforced steel barrier ran parallel to the street. Behind the barrier was a cliff and the rocky beach of the harbor was far below the barrier.

He placed at the ball on the street and rolled it forward. Almost immediately it speeded up, blurring the street. His white sneakers chased it. The girl ran after him. He didn't tell the girl, but he had decided that if her ball rolled toward the barrier he wasn't going to stop it. For if it went over the cliff it meant he had tumor and he was going to die. If he knew he was going to live then he could use hope over time to carry him through his problems one sleepless night at a time, but why bear troubles of living if he was going to die anyway. Why worry about a useless ball.

The ball rolled swerving toward the cliff. It mocked him. He rushed after it. It rolled faster. He caught up to it. Stomped his feet hard on the street next to it. It rushed ahead of him. He became lightheaded. The color of the ball changed from yellow to white to red. It smiled and stayed ahead of him. The ball was happy, uncaring and decadent. The street was spongy. His legs grew tall, then taller. He was dizzy and taller and the blue skies with its white clouds descended on his head and he saw beyond the security of the blue dome into the infinity of the space of death and everything became meaningless.

The ball swerved off the road, and rolled under the barrier. It fell, and kept falling down the granite cliff face. Carlos rushed to the barrier and saw it as it bounced on the stony beach, bounced again and was still. He climbed on top of the barrier. He balanced himself precariously on it. The rushing downward space beckoned him. He felt the oblivion of his death filling the wide-open downward space. It was there - his death was there, tall, ominous and undefined. It hung in the open space and waited, a silent friend. Slowly he began to lean his head forward gradually, deliberately losing his balance to fall irretrievably downward.

"Mister, it's only a ball." The little girl's voice panted.
"It's only a ball. It's only a ball." The words repeated in his head. The closeness of death was seductive. "Yes, and death makes even death meaningless. For after I what is there and if we weren't here who would be here?"

He jerked himself back. His left foot slipped, he fell and for a second he hung there between the nothingness of oblivion and the street on the hill overlooking the town with its ceaseless movement of people, its labyrinth of streets defined by the houses built with entrances and exits and passageways that led to other rooms and other entrances and other exits.

In that second, he realized that nothing can justify life but life itself and there was nothing else available for there was nothing after death, nothing, not even the realization of nothing.

He fell and his buttocks hit the barrier and he found himself straddling the barrier.

He climbed off it and stood on the street. The girl held his hand. "Come," she said. They walked uphill.

"You're going to get me a ball, right?"

"Yeah, it's only a ball,".

They both laughed. Its only a ball. They chatted as they walked uphill in the morning.

A WINDOW'S VIEW OF A HILL

Half an hour later when she opened the door and stepped into the verandah, he walked toward her. It was the first day of September. August had ended with an air of expectation leaving the sea moody and restless. Dark clouds covered the sun and darker clouds of an interminable squall hung in the grey sky in the east over the sea. He knew that as September wore on he would become increasingly conscious of the length of his body and the extensions of his copper arms and legs. He also knew no one would notice that he was distracted, for his full lips were always slightly parted which gave his brown eyes a look of perpetual amazement and innocence.

That morning, the sea had come in. It covered the coral beach and the beach was white under the water and the water was a dull green above the white sand under the dark sky. The sea swelled and tossed and the men pulled the fishing boats up next to the wooden houses and the

earth was soggy and the grass and the trees and the houses were wet. The village smelled of the sea and the scent of fish and the tar and ocum from the lengths of wood of the fishing boats, and the men hung around the rum shops and the billiard table in Smith's shop. They drank and argued, told lies and played billiards for twenty five cents and sometimes for a dollar.

He had seen her yesterday, on the first day in September, standing in front of the large white house on the hill when he had just awoken and the morning was without mood and she stood tall and slender in front of the white house on the hill at the end of the beach.

He stood on the bare floor between the rumpled bed and the window wearing only white cotton underwear. She was framed in the window's view of the hill her head leaned to one side like a child.

He saw the wind ruffle her oversized shirt and lift the broad glow of yellow cloth. She spun with the wind, laughed and said something to someone behind her as she held the skirt down against the force of the wind , and then she looked at the place where the shirt covered her stomach and stopped laughing and looked at the horizon. His eyes followed hers over the mysterious cavity in the world that was filled with the broad liquid sea. It seemed then that she didn't see the water but was standing in the centre of the excitement and dismay of some future expectation.

He walked up the hill toward her when she opened the door the next day and stepped into the verandah wearing white shorts and an oversized red blouse.

Yesterday, looking at her standing, he reached for the blank white sheets and the green pencil that lay on the wooden table next to his rumpled bed. He found himself becoming anxious, anticipatory then expectant as he traced her outline with the thin point of the pencil.

The first year at the University was over. All year as he filled his mind with information to regurgitate on exam booklets, he had ignored the images that flashed in his mind, images which before he sketched or painted, now the surface of his mind had become tense with ideas and the images did not rise into the latticed surface of his consciousness.

During the month of August, he sketched the empty expanse of sea and the straight line of the sea's distant horizon.

He sketched the coral beach, the line of Casurina trees on the hill, and the tourists with their tanned bodies of soft, phospherescent copper, lying on the yellow sand, but one after another he crumpled the sketches in his palm and kept only a white sheet with the single watercolour line of the sea's distant horizon.

As he walked uphill toward her, he found himself becoming expectant. She sat swaying in the white rattan chair. The chair was suspended from a rope in the roof and she was sitting looking out at the sea.

Now thinking of it, he realized that when he walked by the white house on the hill a week ago and heard the music in the darkened air, that made him look at the lighted curtain in the window, that it was her he saw behind the curtain that diffused the light, darkened the details of her naked body leaving only a mobile dark silhouette dancing in a room filled with light. She seemed to be dancing in front of a mirror but then she turned and faced the curtained window. Now as he walked toward her, he was embarrased at the thought that she may have seen him looking at her. That evening after he saw the dancing silhouette, before he entered the silent passage of sleep, he agonized for the dark form, imagining the firm mango weight of her breasts and the roundness of her buttocks rising firmly and filling his palm.

Now she looked at him in the daylight of the overcast sky of the smooth grey morning, as he walked uphill on the narrow street toward her. It seemed she smiled slightly. The wind was blowing uphill. He was thinking that he never saw the wind, didn't know its boundaries. He wondered about the difference between imagination and memory and imagined that the wind was flat and wide and the schools of silver fish were dark in the water and realized that for the first time since August he was not unhappy.

ANOTHER SUN

Tonight after the turmoil of their courtship, after they
were forever married, Bartholomew looked at his wife Qunita
with Maroon's arm about her waist and contemplated his
death. Now he saw her hands of black plastic and remembered
her sitting when he saw her for the first time while he was
washing the salt wind of the Caribbean voyage from his pale
body he noticed her soft brown hands and shy smile her face
fluid with the dark mobile shadows of green leaves and
patches of copper sunshine in the bright shade of a sun that
tossed splashes of red roses in a garden of wild yellow flowers
and and he walked toward her, crushing the bodies that bled
under the weight of the leprosy of his greed, then he had stood

over her and asked to read the lines of laughter in the palms of her brown hands, but tonight after the turmoil of their courtship, now after their marriage of four hundred and thirty years covered in tossed buckets of blood he saw her standing there across from where he sat on the rum shop's icebox next to the machete on the wall and he couldn't hear what she was saying for she was shrouded in the dim light, her head against Maroon, tall, black and drinking from an empty bottle of Coco-Cola, but he heard her laughter as she held Maroon's hand interlacing her fingers of black plastic in his moving their hands behind her back as the barkeeper dressed in a soiled white apron walked toward the icebox his stare moving closer to Bartholomew until he looked Bartholomew full in the face and sneered and yes and I feel your stare you fat barkeeper with your curly mulatto kinks and I heard the castaway standing with his arm around my wife of forever order from you rum and coconut water, yes tonight I have felt the sideways edge of your small eyes probing me asking why don't you grab the machete hanging there next to you and burst his head open because he stands next to your wife of forever whose blood is eternally mingled with yours whose nose is now reshaped like mine and our skin is bleached and brown by the centuries of our illicit love. Forget all that put down the glass, reach for the machete, split the castaway's head open.

Bartholomew held the bitter glass of rum and water in front of him between his palms and over the circle of glass he looked at his past that stretched out flat ahead of him and he felt as if he had been walking backward all his life to get to this place in the shop on the icebox, and he remembered himself as a young man stepping forward into the odorless blue winds of the mornings of his youth filled with the brightness of the newborn sun that never set but held a permanent space in the firmament of his chest.

- Excuse me.

The barkeeper's shoulder brushed against him, Bartholomew avoided his eyes, stood up from the icebox and moved aside, the barkeeper stepped past him and reached for the machete.

Bartholomew looked at Quinata who had aged eight times, eight times became an old woman with lines and blotches and dull grey skin barely hanging unto life and then renewed herself into a young girl with bright black eyes and a blatant optimism there she stood in the dim light of the open rumshop with its tables and chairs its smell of liquor and he remembered the night of the fake Seaport that was built on the mouth of the river where the river flowed into the sea and the sea flowed into the river leaving that place of the world undecided with tides rushing nowhere, making it comfortable for the young who came in the late afternoon bringing the excitement with them from the burning, brilliant unsetting sun that filled their groins and blazed in their faces burning all night and making the night shine like the day so that they spent all night and into the next morning drinking and dancing there among the Seaport's bars, its grey lengths of wooden planks and neon lights and its water that rushed nowhere.

Maroon looked at Bartholomew, saw the sorrows in the memories of his eyes and ignored the distant blank stare that he knew had lost the meaning of the world, for Bartholomew's eyes took everything in without rearranging it, and although Maroon knew Bartholomew was dying he also knew that such men could remain in their distant silence and lunge forward with a machete.

Bartholomew's saddened grey eyes re-emerged from his

memories and he found them looking at Quinata and Maroon who had since sat down and he saw that Quinata was now dressed in green with a red sash and her pale arms had darkened into a glossy black like her perfect heart shaped face with its beak nose like mine and large excited eyes black eyes with glints of blue which were sensual and curious and listening to Maroon against the liquid dimness that shaded her as she sat in the foreground of the mural that covered the wall painted with pirate ships and faded green sugar plantations cut through by brown dirt roads and black Africans turned into machetes loading decapitated stalks of sugar cane tied in bundles into shaky jackass carts and in the mural was painted the vanished half-naked Caribs who welcomed Columbus holding their babies which he murdered against their naked chests.

Bartholomew's eyes turned again to the machete then to Quinata who was sipping rum and coke and he recalled the next day, the day after the last night at the Seaport when this sun burned all night and into the next morning when he sat on his bed in his New York apartment getting dressed pulling on his socks half listening to the newsreader on the television, looking out the window at the blue sun of the new day. He remembered too that when he was brushing his teeth and his back was turned that the odorless yellow wind of the new morning blew past him and took the forty years of his past life with it leaving him new and naked and old.

He had dressed quickly against his urge to lay back, to retire and stay at home. The sun and the wind of the new day was already blowing yellow taxi cabs and people along the streets and toward restaurants in search of coffee and sandwiches. He recalled stepping outside and although it was late he caught up with sun and the wind. But that afternoon as he walked home he noticed for the first time that the wind had become listless and had changed the direction of the day.

The next morning he awoke up oddly abstracted for the morning sun no longer filled him but seemed as far from him as the distance he spent catching up with it the day before and he realized that he was getting old that was when he came with the colonists to St. Cortez, a land without roads to experience rage again to murder the naked Indians and slake his thirst with blood and then he married Quinata for with her he was able to touch the sun again.

So now as he watched Quinata he tasted his jealousy and sipped on the tight, bitter taste of rum and water and he stared from her to the dark cold machete in the barkeeper's hand cutting through the yellow husks of the coconut and then the clouds of the hurricane darkened the day made it personal reduced the space around them and the wind hit against the sides of the shop shaking open the freezer bringing to life the lengths of dead fish, frozen vegetables and packaged meat.

He rushed to the freezer and sat on it. His weight holding the lid down from the storm with its many winds and wild rushing rain.

A skinny Grenadian rushed into the rumshop and said that the immigration officials had come to look for him to deport him but he saw them from on top Union Jack Hill and hid.

Bartholomew put his hand in his pocket and offered the man an American dollar. Someone in the shop shouted above the thunder of the hurricane that the Grenadian had gotten paid that afternoon. Bartholomew gave him the dollar anyway, and when the winds had passed and the shop stopped shaking he returned to his seat on the icebox.

The shopkeeper gave the coconut to Maroon who was still holding on to the table and Quinata to steady himself. The coconut was filled with soft white thick jelly with little water.

The rain drizzled and twelve dark men entered the rumshop. They removed their grey felt hats from their black suits with black shirts and black ties.

They had come from the funeral of Saga Quarts, their friend who when he was alive drank, staggered, talked, argued, who when he was alive drank, staggered, talked, argued and fought with them and they with him and they told him their troubles and he told them his as the years passed and they watched each other get older in the disordered rumshop, with its moody smell of alcohol and cigarettes, and now after the funeral, after walking solemnly and slowly toward the cemetery in two sad uneven lines through the middle of the town behind the dark suits and white dresses and the flowers in the lapels and hands of the mourners folded in front of them following the black hearse with its high black back and black curtained windows that hid the silent dark coffin from the public view they released his body with prayers and hymns into the warm brown earth, to the white maggots and the final darkness and the beginning of the memories.

Now they had come to the rumshop to call his soul back to them to have him there among them and among the ghosts of past friends and pale ancient pirates with their red bandannas and flintlock pistols who had been killed and whose souls were left behind to guard treasures now lost, and to call his soul back into the warm old presence of African ancestors now caught in the stains and crevices of the unpainted wooden boards of the bar and tables amidst the talk and the laughter and the smell of alcohol and the bargaining and gossip the sorrows of generations of patrons yet to come and go.

The twelve dark men ordered a bottle of strong, colorless rum and began drinking from clear small glasses. They continued until they were too dark and abstracted to be sure whether their dear friend had died. Now their thoughts stumbled and blurred unable to conceive of the actualness of death and then they began to talk of their dead friend as though he was there among them and so they began to call him back, waking him up, releasing him from the purgatory of the nothingness of death bringing him back among them into the shop among old friends for they did not want him to be called back only by his widow's mourning, to be caught in the laces on the black bosom of her funeral dress or in the white creases of her tearful handkerchief and so they shared with her the weight of the empty space so she wouldn't call him back only to relive with her over and over again old memories watered down by time and the sadness of her grieving the faint memories of their youthful pleasures that he would enjoy recalling but she would hardly remember, for they were lost from her in the effort and care of worrying about the bruises and fevers of their seven boys and one girl, and her cursing him for the many women he slept with, that she never forgave him for even after the women had grown old with wrinkled and shadowed faces and became different people, he only spent his waiting hours with her when their children had grown into their own lives and the presence of the younger people made them feel meaningless and he could no longer raise the desire for the pleasure of their softening and listless flesh which had once allowed him to tolerate the burden of her moods for as they grew older he had returned to being a small boy with his lack of tolerance for girls and she unable to let go of her absent children and the responsibility she never had for giving purpose to their lives, tried to relieve herself of the burden of his constant sagging presence, his unbuttoned shirt, his baggy soiled pants and worn carpet slippers and his habit of wrapping his cold feet at night in the dirty blacket, she had tried to make him over to change him into the pink plastic doll with the blond hair and glassy blue eyes she had owned when she was a girl whose activities she organized whose hair she combed and whose dresses she decided on, and he in turn would threaten to throw her closet of old dresses through the window if she did not stop trying to change him into a child and then for a moment the brief flame of conflict would burn and she would curse him for his spent love affairs as though they were new.

So gradually he escaped her and spent more time drinking
in the rumshop among the other boys his own age.

Now that he was gone she would sit alone and slowly
digest the empty space that was filled with his presence. So
the men came in their black suits and black hats to give
him a place to come to when he tired of lying on the memories
of her bosom or when he was displaced by her tremors for a
lover.

They had not wanted to leave him in the church either for
the pale blue of its vaulted roof its pious hymns on Sunday
mornings and the ceramic statues of immobile saints standing
in cubicles along the wall to whom he would try to talk and
who would regard him with their silence and their single
unchanging expression which would only remind him that he
was dead.

Neither did they want to leave him in the uncomfortable
spaces of the new rumshops with plastic seats and hard
formica table tops with fake wood patterns where the new
young gathered with their loud frantic music.

So they called him back to the rumshop with its old songs,
its moody smell of rum and cigarettes and the scent of lengths
of salted codfish and brown burlap bags of sugar and old
calendars and dunning receipts of wires hanging overhead and

the coming and going of townspeople and the laughter of the children.

Miss Princess, the townswoman who had bathed his corpse held the hairs of the back of his head in her hand between her fingers and silently soaped the still and empty face, which expressed in fallen lines the attitude he adopted toward the ironies of life, came into the shop dressed in white with purple flowers. She passsed by where Bartholomew sat.

The shopkeeper put a glass on the counter for her and she drank one drink with the men then another and she embraced them and they shared their dark purple sadness through the spaces of the white bones of their chests and then she said goodbye and left them.

Bartholomew put the cold glass of rum and water to his lips swallowed it and got up, for his presence seemed inappropriate at the ritual of the mourners of the man to whose funeral he had not gone.

As he stood he pushed his hands in his pocket in search of a dollar and he noticed that his wife Quinata and Maroon had left.

He walked from the shop into the rain along Harbour Street peering through the broad glass windows of the new bars and he saw his wife in the dim lights of Club Maria. She was talking and intently relaxed with her back on the back of the chair and her feet firmly on the floor.

Two young men sat with her in the dark mahagony surroundings with its bright neon beer signs and the tinkle of glass and the formica table tops with designs of fake wood. So he continued walking through the night and into the morning until he fell asleep and went in a dream to his sister's house in Maine where he found Maroon standing tall in front of the door blocking his path.

Bartholomew told him to move but Maroon stood there silently and Bartholomew said again,

- Move, either go in or out. For I am going to close the door.

Maroon moved and Bartholomew stepped into the house where his sister was wrapped in a towel. She had asked her husband to move out and she was about to shower and her small son was dressed for school in a uniform with a red tie with white diagonal lines.

He went to the bathroom and knelt in front of the white ceramic tub and cried loosing the burden of his sorrows breaking it into thick white clots of mucus that clogged his chest, then sadly he stepped under the shower and the waters washed them away.

Then he woke from his dreams and found that he had been asleep in a shallow gutter on the side of the street that led to their house. He got up and walked home his clothes soaked against his skin.

Quinata was not home when he got there and he walked through the house and packed her things in plain pillow cases and then he put them in front of the door knowing she would never return and he showered again and dressed and walked toward the rumshop.

part II - in an american setting

OCTOBER

It was warm this morning but the sky was bleak and grey, as though it was going to rain, and a chill, the murky grey chill of winter was in the morning.

And he remembered the summer. Its untamed optimism, the white spinning sun, scintillating radiant light on a blue lake. He recalled the delirious infinity of light and the luminous sweat hot on his forehead and the kiss of first love. A dizzy skyward rush, from flaming green fields into an infinity of brilliant light.

It heated up as the day wore on. It became warm and brilliant, but he remembered the dismal morning, the bleak grey of the wilted sun. And he was lost like an old man among his memories. Drooping memories like the wet brown and yellow leaves falling slowly on the sidewalk in the dismal rain. Wet brown and yellow leaves that could not be pinned back to their branches to live again the summer to love again the sunshine.

Sometimes in the morning he sees her. She is tall. She doesn't know he sees her. She carries a bag over her right shoulder and walks with unhurried steps, hands in the pockets of a grey trenchcoat. Her close cropped hair is sprinkled with grey. Her face is pleasant, dark, sweet - was once good looking, and bags like tears under her eyes.

Her eyes are usually focused on her thoughts and her afro with its sprigs of grey gives her the dignity of having avoided the desperation that appears in dyed hair above wrinkled faces.

He saw her that morning. The crisp rhythm of her yellow high heels hurried over the wet, brown and yellow leaves.

She was wearing a black leather jacket flared open at the front. Her large motherly breasts pushed against the buttons of her blouse. She wore a tight pair of red pants and as she hurried her soft, round buttocks danced, naked below the panty lines.

It was a cold grey morning - that morning with a grey chill in the air but they said it would be sunny, hot for that time of year.

LEGS

It was rumored that the guy walking toward Shanta sold homicides and dope. She recognized him, remembered his name, Hard Rock. A sneer tightened her face. She glanced away and took a quick pull on her cigarette. Dania sat next to her in the restaurant. She did not mention him to Dania. Dania continued leafing through the copy of a woman's magazine. 'What's happened to our men?' she asked herself.

In the corner of her eye, through the restaurant's broad panel glass, she saw Hard Rock cross the street, coming toward them on tense elongated legs. Shanta steadied her elbow on the table and placed her fist under the chin of her plain yellow face. She looked at Dania, admired the black, smooth, beauty of her soft chisled features, and the cigarette between her fingers became a slim burning spear protecting her and Dania from the world.

They had made love that morning. It was August and hot, but in the apartment the fan was on and they lay soft and close, four breasts, they tasted each other, parted tangled hairs, and it had ended as usual with Dania's head resting between Shanta's small breasts as she parted and stroked her hair.

Dax was with them in the restaurant. He was tall, dark, athletic and casually well dressed. He waited at the counter for the waitress to place their order on a tray so he could take it over to the girls.

Hard Rock came up to the restaurant. He glanced quickly and cleanly through the panel glass with its big yellow lettering that read 'West Indian Food'. His eyes flashed on the patrons, the red and white checkered table cloths, the steam rising from pots of hot curried meats. Grey smoke curled slowly upward from the hot tip of Shanta's cigarette.

A blue city bus with sunglass windows stopped at the red light, a line of cars extended behind it like a dusty, multicolored tail. Hard Rock felt the waiting eyes of the passengers. He arranged himself in sharp, red geometrical lines swaggered and pulled his Yankees baseball cap down sideways over the left eye of his small tight head. The black, torn streets of Brooklyn cut through the disorder of unwashed red brick buildings. He stepped into the restaurant rolling his shoulders and hips, modeling tension, his open palms in front of his crotch.

"Sadness and craziness," Shanta thought.

He moved to where Shanta sat. Dania looked up from the magazine. Shanta felt him pause behind her. Dania reached for her purse. The tension came, tightening the muscles of her back. Shanta held the tension stiff in her shoulders and the back of her head. Anger squinted her eyes. Hard Rock moved past them. Shanta breathed out, then they accepted his presence in the restaurant and avoided looking at him.

Behind them a Spanish woman with black hair and a sharp nose sat with her two sons. She wore a red and yellow dress. Hard Rock moved toward her table.

Dax turned to the girls. He saw Hard Rock with the lines of aggression quivering on his face painted in tense, metallic silver-black. Dax knew him. At Samuel McKay High School he had threatened Dax with a knife. Dax had asked him if he had done his homework.

Dax watched as Hard Rock walked to the Spanish woman's table and began to pull his pants and underwear down. The woman stood up. "Mira, esta maricon. No lo puedo creer," she said and grabbed her boys' arms and moved over to where Dax stood.

Hard Rock jumped on the table, squatted and began to shit brown and heavy, then he wiped himself with the table cloth, stood up tall on the table, legs spread apart, pulled up his pants, zipped his fly, and jumped from the table.

He was sauntering through the door when Shanta and Dania heard popping sounds like bottles of champagne opening. Two bullets slammed into Hard Rock's face and chest jerking him backward. He fell with a dull thud in the doorway.

Shanta and Dania turned. They saw a man dressed in dark clothes running down the block and the blood forming into a thick pool around Hard Rock's body. They saw his red geometrical lines sag, become pale, blue and soft. The world was silent, huge and monumental about the corpse as Hard Rock became still, and silent and monumental and dead. The four other persons in the restaurant had stopped eating. They spoke quietly.

One of the boys standing with his mother got up and rushed toward Hard Rock. She grasped at him and shouted, "No, Alfredo." He shrugged her grasp from his shoulder, rushed toward the huge corpse took off Hard Rock's Yankee baseball hat, placed it sideways on his head and stepped into the street sauntering on tense elongated legs arranged in sharp red, geometrical lines, hustling tension with clean, sharp glances.

On the restaurant's radio, the news reader was saying, "Recent Gallup polls show Black candidate Johnson Brown III leading in the democratic primaries ..."

At the back of the store, the restaurant owner stepped from behind a brown unpainted door. He had a huge sullen face. His lower lip pushed down by a half smoked cigar. It made his huge paunch appear tough. He wiped his hands on a soiled white apron covering his paunch, took up the table cloth, held it away from him, stepped carefully over Hard Rock's corpse, walked outside and dumped the table cloth in the garbage cannister on the sidewalk. When he came back he took off the soiled apron and covered the corpse and the body below it became even more silent and still.

The news reader continued, "Johnson Brown III's position as frontrunner is due to the fact that Tom Collony was forced to drop out of the race because of his role in the embezzlement scandal ..."

"Something smells bad in here," Dania said.

"Must be the bums outside," Shanta replied.

The waitress placed the Spanish woman's order in a tray on the counter. She took the tray of fried fish and chips without looking at it. She now had only one boy. She took him to a table in the back and sat down. They looked through the restaurant's window.

Shanta stood up.

"C'mon let's leave," Dania said.

The waitress put the plates of steaming curried goat and rice on the counter.

"We're leaving," Dax told her.

"Well pay for the food then."

"We don't want it."

"You order it. I serve it, so you ain't must pay for it."

Dax was starting to argue.

Shanta said, "Take it Dax. It's bad luck to step over a corpse anyway."

In the distance the uncoming ambulance wailed mechanically. Gradually its wailing overwhelmed everything.

Dax looked around the restaurant. No one was eating nor moving. They spoke quietly. Shanta turned and looked casually at the small crowd gathering outside.

Dax brought over the trays of food. Shanta saw Dania smile and roll her eyes at Dax, she didn't say anything. She quickly turned back to the crowd. When Dax went for the glasses of juice Dania saw Shanta studying her carefully.

"Maybe he won't want what you got," Shanta said, an edge in her voice.

"C'mon Shanta, I have, I mean don't have ... Shut up Shanta."

Shanta looked at her coolly and looked away. She had begun to hate Dax. They had met him at the writers' workshop and he had unsettled her on the first day. Just as Dania had when she first saw her, just like her ex-husband had too. But the unsettling she felt when Dax came had been edged by an anxiety which increased after he had read four of his poems.

When Shanta met Dania, Dania had been Nel's lover. Shanta won Dania from Nel. Her strategy was simple. Dania wanted to be a writer but was having problems. Shanta was very attentive to her. It didn't help Dania's writing.

Shanta felt it was because Dania had closed off some level of herself, someplace where she was vulnerable. But Shanta praised even her worse work and spent a lot of time with her. Nel stopped talking to Shanta. Eventually their relationship made Nel angry and jealous. At a New Year's party she slapped Dania twice. That night Shanta and Dania drove home together.

Shanta had used this method with at least four other women in the workshop. Even with those who had boyfriends, she was sensitive and attentive, reminding them that women needed to help and heal each other, for sooner or later men brought pain and you could only trust them but so much. Her prediction always came true and each time it did, she comforted the women, hugged them, became more intimate. She involved herself in their work showing them new techniques and possibilities of plot, character and theme that they had overlooked. Gradually the women lost confidence in their art and felt unable to work without her help for the work was no longer theirs but hers also. Then she would criticize their best work and praise their bad work leaving them confused and dependent.

Bianca was the workshop leader. A pleasant heavy set older woman who wore an afro, and had learned to accept the routines of the world. When men showed up at the workshop, Shanta insulted even their best work and the other women took their cue from her.

The insulted men hardly came back. So, gradually a citadel of women sat around Shanta and eventually she became convinced that she was better for all women than any of the "dicks and balls".

When Dax came to the workship with his tall good looks, silent eyes, and small round ass, she found herself thinking of her own tall, yellow body, her small breasts, her face which she thought was too long. He read and the women applauded spontaneously, she applauded too and whispered under her

breath "Fuck him!" and after that she wasn't so sure of
herself.

Now as Dax brought the trays of food over, she felt
threatened. As he rested the tray down, she reached under
table, placed her hand on Dania's leg and caressed it, glancing
at Dax to see if he saw, but he had turned away and was
walking back to the counter. "Shanta, quit it." Dania slapped
her hand away.

Outside, the traffic lights were red again. The cars
stopped and more people were gathering.

Dax returned. Dania took out her compact and put on
fresh lipstick. Dax noticed the burdened silence between the
women. They looked at the food and looked away. The corpse
reminded them that they were eating flesh. Shanta looked at
Dax and smiled sweetly.

"Today is a good day for the beach," he said.

He took a roll of mints from his pocket and offered the
women. Shanta took one. "I can get accustomed to treatment
like this," she said. "My mother warned me about men like
you. Beach too, eh. Soon I'll be dusting sand from my back."

Dax smiled and raised his eyebrows. This wasn't like
Shanta. She always carried her wall and her lighted cigarette
with her. As far as he knew she was not the type to play and

neither was he treating her special. Shanta had paid for her order.

"Well I know a place on you where you won't get sand," Dax said. Shanta laughed. Dax laughed but Dania didn't. Shanta ignored her.

"You've got to show me where." Shanta smiled.

The cops came, then the ambulance came, wailing. The cops took photographs and asked if anyone saw what happened. No one answered. The ambulance left with the corpse and the proprietor came back through the unpainted door wearing a clean white apron and carrying a mop and a bucket of water mixed with ammonia. He began to swab the doorway. The smell of ammonia was stronger than the fresh scent of the blood. When he was done and the doorway was clean, everyone got up and left.

That evening Dax was reading in his book-cluttered apartment when Dania called on the phone. They were talking about the hot weather and foreign films when Dania dared him to guess what she was wearing. He paused.

"You're naked."

She giggled, "No, I'm wearing socks." After that they talked about trivial things and decided to go out together that Friday. When she hung up, Dax felt a pleasant space in his chest and a dense solidity in his crotch.

"Black, sweet and beautiful Dania."

The phone rang. He answered it quickly.

"You were just talking to Dania, weren't you?"
Shanta asked.

"Why?" he asked.

"Well I phoned both of you and both lines were busy."

"Yeah, we were chatting. She's quite nice."

There was silence at the other end.

"Listen," Shanta said, "why don't you come over. I've got a
bottle of champagne. Let's talk and get silly."

Now he was puzzled. "You're sure that's you Shanta?"

"Of course it's me," she laughed

"What are you smoking?"

"Nothing. Stop it. Tonight I want to screw and I like you,
simple."

"Serious?"

"C'mon Dax," she said softly. "You know what the deal
is."

"What deal?"

Shanta was quiet. After a long moment, she said, "listen,
I've got work to do."

She hung up Dax was perplexed.

Shanta was initiating the tryst. He lay back on the couch, stared at the ceiling and found it interesting.

'She's willing to let me lay her without any effort on my part. Obviously she's opening a space ahead of me, come into my parlor said the spider to the fly, she was going to pull me into that space. But the space would be her space; she knew what this is all about. I don't. But what space and why?'

Dax stood up, walked to the refrigerator, took out a can of cola and told himself 'you think too much'. He opened the can. "Maybe she liked me all along but only showed it after she sensed Dania was interested." He felt flattered. The cola was light and sweet in his mouth. He thought of it some more, imagining Shanta's stern face and again he became wary.

As he sipped the soda, he realised that he preferred pursuit because he felt that when the woman gave in she was emotionally snared at some level and he had some control of the space. 'It protects me' he thought 'from the humiliation of being told at four in the morning, okay, you're done now, so put on your clothes and get lost.'

Now he felt insulted that she had chosen him to make the offer to.

That Friday after work, Dania and Dax met amidst the mahogany and polished glass at the bar of the Barbizon Hotel.

Dania drank wine. He drank Chinese beer. The people around them chatted. They talked about camera angles in foreign films. The alcohol blurred the distance between them. She had charming happy eyes, smiling, leaning forward toward him over the dark marble table top. Then they left Barbizon and went to Alo Alo to eat. At midnight they were walking along Lexington to 53rd holding hands, talking, they turned left and headed for Roseland discoteque. The music swirled them and they kept it with them. Moving it with the twists and turns of their bodies.

Five thirty a.m., half drunk, spaced, tired, and happy they waited on Broadway for a taxi and saw the young Puerto Rican with the yankee's cap. He sauntered by on tense elongated legs arranged in red lines, modeling tension. Dax's eyes followed him. Dania waved at an oncoming taxi. It stopped. They got in and rode to his place.

She had her chin on his shoulder and her arms around him as he opened the door. The phone was ringing.

"Don't answer it," Dania whispered in his ear as she walked clumsily behind him into the apartment, her arms wrapped around his waist.

All through the day, he smelled her perfume and could feel her soft weightless body on his chest.

When he called her that evening, she was not home. He called Shanta's and her answering machine was on.

The next day he called Dania at work. The receptionist said that she was on a week's vacation.

He called her the next two nights, she was not home and Shanta's machine was still taking messages.

She was home that Friday. He called and asked her out.

"Where?"

"Freddie Hubbard is playing at the Blue Note."

She agreed and he asked her where the hell was she.

"Out in the country."

"Why didn't you say something ... "

"My, my, we are getting possessive, aren't we?"

"Was Shanta with you?"

"Yeah. Why?"

"Nothing, her machine was on."

"Oh."

At the club, the jazz and the wine made them smooth and blank. They smiled and fitted into each other's presence lightly, then they went home to her place and made love.

On Saturday, Dania came to the writers' workshop. Dax noticed a scratch on her cheek and a smudge of lipstick over her lip.

"Fighting with your compact?" he asked.

She smiled and rubbed her leg against his under the table. Chavon, who kept her intelligence disguised by a clown's smile was reading a fantasy tale about blue Martians when Shanta walked through the door. Shanta was wearing jeans and a broad black leather belt which rested of the illusory rise of her backside. She walked over to where Dania and Dax were sitting and sat on the other side of Dax. Dania got up and sat in another seat. Shanta ignored her. Chavon continued reading, her bright eyes appeared innocent, unfortified.

Shanta nudged Dax's arm. He didn't respond. He was angry at her. He looked over at Dania. Shanta passed him a note. Why was she so damn annoying. He read, 'The bubbly is still unopened. What's up?' he felt her crowding him.

He wrote below her note. 'OK, keep it bubbling.'

Chavon finished reading the fantasy tale. The workshop was silent for a moment. Bianca called on Grace to begin the critique. "I liked it. I really did ..."

Shanta nudged Dax arm again and passed him another note. It read "It's not OK that I can't pull the cork."

He shook his head and smiled. She winked. He caught

Dania looking at him.

Shanta was scheduled to read that day and when it was her turn, she cleared her throat and began.

The story was about a strong and singularly lazy man. He liked drinking beer on the corner, out of brown paper bags. After which he went home and forced his woman to go to bed with him. The woman worked and paid the bills but he stopped her from talking to friends on the phone, stopped her from having friends over and "persistently put his fist in her face."

When his woman had had it with that crap, she took a shotgun and blew a hole in him "as big as the other side of a barn." And, Shanta continued, "every year on the anniversary of the murder she went to his grave to squeeze the dirt between her fingers and drew strength from it for the coming year.

The story ended. Shanta reached for a pen to write the comments and the critique of the group.

"I like it. I really liked it," a woman with a close chopped afro began. Chavon got up and left the room. Dax walked after her. He found her looking out of a window at the green spaces of the park. She was wearing an oversized white shirt and washed out blue jeans. Her rasta braids framed the side of her face.

"I see you liked Shanta's story." She turned around, saw Dax and smiled.

"It was O.K. I guess, but shit it's scary."

"Same story over and over again." "Yes, no, but the problem is real," Chavon added. "When a man hits us what do we say? He didn't mean it, or he hit me because he was in pain, or it was really my fault. Do you know what that says? It says that there are times when abuse is valid. We say it, yeah women do. But sooner or later we catch onto that game and say, you know what, I didn't respect myself, that's why I said that crap. This man is kicking my ass and I'm gonna get rid of the bastard."

"Scary."

"No, that's not what scares me," said Chavon staring through the window. "What scares me is I think the women may be too messed up to help the men." They were silent. Chavon rested her back on Dax's chest.

"How is the novel coming?" she asked.

"Slowly." Dax paused, then said, "I think Shanta likes me."

"You're always being funny, Dax," Chavon said, not

moving.

"No joking. She's been inviting me over."

Chavon kept looking through the window. "Look Dax. Dania is Shanta's woman or however that goes."

"You mean?"

"Yeah, I mean."

"So that's the deal," Dax said.

"What's the deal?"

Dax was silent.

"Who knows? Maybe she wants you to be her woman." Chavon turned around. They both laughed and walked back to the workshop.

That afternoon Dax called Shanta. He told her he was coming over to open the bubbly. She laughd and said fine.

He drove to her address. She lived in a blue collar, white neighborhood.

He disliked white American neighborhoods. To him they were silent places, hostile places of permanent frost.

As he approached the building in which she lived he saw two white men, large with big necks, dressed in soiled white T-shirts tucked into their pants under the cliffs of their stomachs. They stood on either side of the glass and steel doorway.

"Shit."

The men watched as Dax approached. Simultaneously, they cleared their throats and spat on the concrete walkway.

The blond in the baseball hat walked past them and into the building.

Dax stepped between and past the two men. He pushed the outer door and stepped into the confines of the small rectangular space between the inner and outer doors.

There was an intercom on the wall. he scanned the listing of apartments and the names. 'Shanta's apartment number was 5D. Where was it? Shit."

He looked over his shoulder. The two men had turned and were looking at him. ' ... Jesus Christ, I don't even have a blade.' He tried the inner door. It was locked. He felt trapped.

He turned back to the intercom deciding if those pale motherfuckers made a move, he would gorilla them.

'5D, 5D, where is 5D?' He peered at the list of names next to the intercom. The tension hurried him. His heart was wild and faint.

"Hey nigger, what you want?"

Dax spun around. He pushed his hand under his jacket.

"Who the fuck you talking to?" he said and moved toward

the questioner. Out of the corner of his eyes Dax saw the other guy walk away.

"I was talking to ..." the white guy's voice trailed off but his eyes frozen on the bulge of Dax's hand inside his jacket. He turned and saw his friend walking away. He wiped his lips.

Slowly, Dax pulled his hand out of his jacket. The guy was as still as stone. His eyes staring at the motion under the jacket. Dax's hand came out empty. The guy sighed. Dax stretched his hand. "My name is Saul."

The guy shook Dax's hand automatically. "Nice meeting you, Mister. My name is Tony."

"Com'ere Tony, where is 5D?"

With the tension gone Dax spotted the number. Tony stood staring at the intercom. Dax let him scan the intercom and then said, "O.K. Tony I see it." Dax pushed on the buzzer.

Shanta buzzed him.

"Why do you live in this iceberg. Bet you can't buy a copy of Ebony at the corner newsstand," Dax said stepping into Shanta's apartment.

"No and I don't have roaches either," Shanta answered.

"Yeah! so what did I pass downstairs."

"You probably brought them," Shanta countered.

"What do you know, your hair is boiled in lye."

"And you've got some corn cob up your ass. Relax, take the

load off."

Dax looked at Shanta and smiled. She smiled back. In her red high heels, she towered above him.

With a big girlish sigh she said, "Have a seat, my son's sleeping. I've got the bubbly, wanna drink?"

Her apartment was tastefully decorated, modern, art deco, in grey and blue. A large impressionist painting of a blues trumpeter saddened the wall above a low grey leather couch.

"Where's your son?"

"Tasheem? Oh, he's in bed."

"I'll have the drink."

She waited as he took off his jacket, then took it from him. He sat on the couch below the sad trumpeter, watched her turn and walk away and saw how the pink jumpsuit curved close to her.

She returned with a silver ice bucket, a chilled bottle of champagne stuck in it.

"Open it for me," Shanta said, "I hate popping corks."

Dax took the bottle. She turned her back and shut her eyes tightly and jumped when the cork popped.

Dax poured the champagne. She sat opposite him in another chair, a higher one, crossed her long legs, lit a cigarette and watched him through the smoke.

Dax sipped the wine. "You're like the night, beautiful."

"Stop it. You didn't come here to court me."

"Come sit next to me," Dax said patting the couch.

She didn't move just looked at him. Dax felt like leaving. The skin was close to the angular bones in her long face, but her legs were long, yellow and just fine.

He wondered about her. Was she happy? He didn't think so. What would make her happy? Could he make her happy? He finished the glass of champagne.

"I'm not going into the bedroom until you come over here," he said grinning playfully.

Shanta put out the half burned cigarette and nervously lit another.

"Couch her, then bed her. C'mon Dax, that's old fashioned. Now it's 'I've got mine, to hell with it if you didn't get yours.' "

"Same thing."

"You want me or not," Shanta asked, lighting another cigarette, her hand quivering.

"Why are you nervous, Shanta?"

"Because I don't know you that well Dax."

"You're just saying that because you don't want to ..."

"No, I'm telling you that because the last man I had broke my nose and dislocated my jaw."

"Is that why you want to protect Dania?"

Shanta was quiet. She stared at him got up, walked to the couch, sat next to Dax and looked at him closely. "Why should I protect her?" He refilled her glass from the bottle of champagne.

"I know you're her lover Shanta." Dax was getting angry.

Shanta laughed. "Sure you don't have it mixed up." There was an edge to her laughter. "In that case the deal would be you screw me with all your lust, no cost, no responsibility as long as you leave Dania alone."

"Sounds like an opportunity to vomit on each other," Dax said, getting up and walking toward the door.

"C'mon Dax don't be foolish."

"I'm listening. You like me. I know it. You know it."

"You know that and you're walking through that door, you bastard. You mother fucking nigger bastard," Shanta shouted, lifting her foot and pulling off one of the spiked heel shoes. Dax turned the brass door knob and pulled the door. It didn't open. He felt wind flick pass his ear. Instinctively he shifted his face. Shanta's red shoe hit the door. It bounced and the metal edge of the heel hit him under the right eye. He spun around, his hand reached up to his face. There was blood on his fingers.

Shanta rushed toward him. Her arms encircled him. He

tried to shrug her off but she held on.

She rested her head on the back of his shoulder and began crying softly. Blood fell in her hair.

He turned around in her arms and found her standing lopsided in one shoe and taller than him. She held his face against her bossom. The blood smeared her clothing. She bent her head and began to kiss him.

"I think your son is up," Dax said looking past her.

Shanta turned and saw Tasheem peeking from the bedroom door. Tasheem saw his mother wiping her eyes.

Dax released her. She put her shoe on and walked over to the frightened child, towering over him.

"It's O.K. honey. Mommy is fine. Go back to sleep."

He stared past her at Dax with big, frightened, sad eyes. Dax smiled at him. "Hi Tasheem."

Tasheem ran to him mommy and held her about her leg.

Shanta took him back to his room and came back smoking. She walked over to Dax squinting through the cigarette smoke. He took her hand and led her to the bedroom. The light of the street lamps was silent coming through the curtain. He removed her jumpsuit. Her yellow skin glowed dim in the light of the street lamp. She began to remove his pants then stopped and cooly sauntered past him walking toward the living room on tense legs. He lay on the bed, relaxed and expectant. He thought he heard Dania's voice. Shanta came back in naked and smoking, cooly eyeing him again, squinting through the smoke.

"Put out the cigarette girl."

"I'm nervous," she said laying next to him. He rolled over and lay on her. Her body was soft and warm and yellow under his. He took the cigarette from her and put it out in the ash tray on the side table next to the bed. His wet tongue and moist lips moved down her stomach. She lit up another cigarette and blew a mouthful of slow smoke rings.

He kissed her. She blew smoke rings into his mouth and he tasted the salt of her tears through the sides of his lips.

She moved slowly at first, past the tightness, past the thick fit, looking up at him. There was a welt under his right eye. The agony of her pleasure moaned her and merged her with him. The cigarette burned in the ashtray. She left it there and when the colors came thundering deep blue and purple waves, she shouted and moaned "Bastard" and dug her nails in him. "Stop. Stop, you bastard. Oh God no. Nooo."

He didn't hear the door open. She shuddered and subsided lying back on the pillow.

Her leg was resting over his back when the light came on

white and blinding. He squinted, hurting the cut under his eye. Through the pressure of the light he looked at the door and saw Dania standing there. From behind Dania's leg, Tasheem looked at his mother.

Dania's head was bent to one side, her face expressionless, just staring at him.

"Get to bed Tasheem."

Dax rolled over and pulled the sheet.

Shanta got up. Her naked body vulnerable in the bright light. She was crying when she walked toward Dania. "Why didn't you come earlier Dania. You were there in Tasheem's room. You knew ..." Shanta wiped her eyes.

"What do you think of him now Dania?" Shanta walked around the bed, got a cigarette and lit it.

She bent and picked up Dax's pants and threw it for him.

"Here."

Dax stood, naked, black, muscular. The welt and cut under his eye, the sweat on his skin. He looked at Dania. Shanta looked at him. Dania said, "Get dressed and get out."

The door was left opened. He stepped through it and walked down the empty dim lit stairs past the brown closed doors of other apartments. His shirt hung out of his pants, the rumpled ends visible below the soft leather jacket.

He was on the landing of the second floor about to step down.

"Dax." A small female voice and hurrying footsteps sounded behind and above him.

TOSSING THE TOSSED DIE

That morning the obituary and a photograph of Jacques, the keeper of the secret diary, 'mistakenly' appeared in *The Times*, identifying him as a heroic intelligence agent who had been killed in a lower Manhattan art gallery by leftist Guatemalan guerillas.

From the time Jacques saw his red, purple and green hairstyle printed in newspaper shades of grey and white and read his obituary beneath the photograph. He pushed his fingers in his hair which was styled with the individual strands standing on end, as though arranged by a bolt of lightning, and rushed over to the louvre blinds in front of the windows of his office in the gallery and closed them, knocking over the chair, shutting out the pale October sunshine, the view of other windows and people rushing toward varied fates.

The act had been a purely instinctual one and when it was done, he stood there stunned racing his now numbed brain trying to find out why he had reacted with such wild suddenness.

"I'm alive, what's ... "

He was about to shrug when the delayed realization came like a time bomb that imploded in his chest, leaving in its wake a faint and vacuous space that enveloped his stomach and crotch. In this void, his dry, weightless balls and entrails floated. His heartbeat quickened. Automatically he dropped to the floor breaking his fall with open palms; jolting the muscles of his shoulder. His round granny glasses fell from his brown face onto the grey carpet. He put the glasses back on, pushed them against his short snubbed nose, then he began to crawl toward the front door using his elbows to pull his long body forward.

Above him hung the flattering abundantly medalled, shiny-eyed, stern-jawed portraits of megalomaniacs that the gallery shipped out to create disorder in the Third World. Jacques crawled around the corner of the L-shaped gallery. Moving as quickly as possible, he got to the door, reached up with his right hand, turned the brass knob and locked the door. Then he reached for the strings of the other louvre

blinds and pulled them shut. His palms felt moist. He pulled himself up to his feet, feeling less secure in the citadel of portraits. The phone rang. He rushed to his desk, picked it up and listened. There was silence, except for the faint sound of tense breathing on the other end. Jacques remained quiet, listening. "C'mon, a whore got your tongue, or what?"

"Oh, it's you."

It was Randall, a short ex-marine boxer with a permanent crewcut. Randall, his assistant in the gallery, friend and a fellow agent.

"Listen, Jacques," Randal said, matter of factly, "I'm not gonna be in today."

"Why, what's the matter?" It was a useless question and Jacques knew it when he asked.

"My cat died. Shit, you wanna know. I'm sorry, Jacques ... well ..."

Then there was an awkward, dented silence between them. In it Jacques could feel Randall's presence as though he was there, in the room, in front of him. Jacques visualized Randall's battered and apologetic face, understood and hung up the phone.

Jacques sat heavily in the high-backed office chair and

with nervous desperation began to thoughtfully arrange cocaine crystals into neat, white lines on the smooth face of his black-lacquered desk.

He removed the glasses from his handsome, long face, snorted the first line,and began to swivel the leather chair in soaring semi-circles, cocaine-confident that he could handle this shit that was going down, but trying to find some other reasonable and convincing explanation for the presence of the photograph.

'Who could have made such a foolish error? Just who could have and why should they have supplied my photo to the newspapers?' He knew he was trying to find a way to lie to himself. That the only mistake that could have been made was that the photo had appeared on the wrong day. Maybe it was to have been printed the following week, for then he was scheduled to be on a mission in Guatemala.

He stared at the photo again. It was him alright. He pushed the newspaper away to the left on the desk next to his usually pocketed, dog-eared and well-traveled diary of clandestine entries. On the first page of that diary was this entry:

I am Jacques. I am a guardian. I guard the mysteries. I am aware that I guard the mysteries. The mysteries exist

behind the definitions. Definitions are cultural explana-
tions of mysteries. Guardians are usually not aware that
they guard mysteries. Most guardians guard definitions
and the mysteries take care of themselves. All
societies have mysteries. They are what allow societies to
continue to be. The mystery is what is hidden by the
definitions people are taught to believe. A few citizens are
not believers. They are dispensable. I am a guardian. I
have erased such.

In the frightened, vacant feeling of his crotch, a drop of
golden urine began to form at the head of his penis. The drop
expanded, became rounded and spongy, then solid and urgent,
softly tickling at his thighs. He got up and walked to the
bathroom, unzipped, and spread his legs, balancing himself in
front of the toilet bowl - a white, oval abstraction in carefully
moulded ceramic containing a silent pool of water. A work of
artistic genius, he thought, and also capable of an all-
important function.

Of course he had been an agent, operating undercover as
an archaeologist. The toilet bowl stared at him. Its water was
calm, expectant. The photograph that appeared in *The Times*
had been taken atop the steps of an ancient Mayan temple. He
stared at the bowl. It waited. No urine was coming. He put his

vacant and flaccid penis back into his pants, didn't zip it up, went back to the office and began again to swivel speedily in his chair.

He had done good as an agent too, managed to penetrate a major rebel group operating in the jungles of Guatemala.

For Jacques, the guerillas were the philosophers of the dying twentieth century operating at a time when words without explosions were not as convincing or important as technology. Some of the guerillas were convinced that Christ was still coming, but Marx had beat him to it. Others argued that it was because Christ had reneged on his promise that Marx showed up. Jacques used to settle the ongoing argument by saying, "Senores, every revolution tries to put Christ and Marx in the same bed."

"Jacques, my son, I wouldn't wish that even on these peons, said Mr. Clark, Jacques' superior on that mission, an oriental with dark yellow skin and a bony, sinister smile, regarded that combination as abominable. Look, Jesus' method of salvation is one of the payoffs for obedience and patience. It includes a perpetual life of indolence in a retirement home on the upper floors of a skyscraper with an eternity of torture for dissenters in the basement. Marx's utopia is one of owned sweat requiring a particular type of cerebration that allows the intellect to invoke opposites and to harmonize them through the belief that God was made of atoms to be distributed according to effort and need. The ends are similar, for Columbus has proved that the earth is circular. A proof that brought about a permanent industry in ankle and neck chains. Maybe that's why Marxists avoid Jesus ..."

Yet, it was mainly his ability to supply the rebels with medicines and bandaged that endeared him to them. And the rebel leader, Carlos, had accepted him telling the guerillas one day as they rested leaning against a Mayan pyramid with its layers of buildings upon buildings, "Jacques he's no gringo. Look, his eyes, they have passion. The passion of a believer."

Jacques' next assignments was to train counter-communist insurgents in Nicaragua. They believed that capitalism proved that Christ had come again in the form of Adam Smith. Thus, they were fighting to liberate the land to allow the invisible hand of God to express itself freely. After two months among them, Jacques had come to accept that they were correct. Again Jacques strengthened his convictions by arguing that Marxism already had its ultimate expression in the North American middle class.

With that memory, Jacques stopped swiveling and lay

back in his chair. He stretched his legs with an air of smug amusement, but sat bolt upright when a thunder of squeals and rattles exploded underground as an IRT train rushed along its subterranean tracks. The vibrations shook his small office door almost visibly. He stared blankly at the door. It looked like the cover of a coffin, the glass at its upper end being the place to view the face of his corpse.

"So what," he said, turning his face away. "We're all already dead sometime in the future." Then he reached across the desk and picked up the secret diary, convinced that the solution to his predicament was to be found among its illicit and unspeakable entries. He opened it impulsively. The page was 28. He read and became fascinated by his own thoughts. The entry he had made four years ago while working as a union organizer in South Africa began:

> *"I am given the function of guardian because they are convinced that I no longer have the capacity to think. Having sung the national anthem and saluted the flag too many times, having grown up in the 'right' neighborhood, and having had the right parents, having eaten baked apples and visited silent natural monuments. Because of this it was considered safe to train me to be. Therefore I was trained to be. To be is to experience one's beingness.*

*One's beingness is always blank. Because of this I can play
many roles. Ask an actor. He will tell you he can be
whomever you hire him to be. I was trained to be like an
actor, to change my sense of beingness to fit whatever role I
was to assume so as to do my job protecting the definitions.
We are chosen carefully, since to play the role of someone
else conditioned by other definitions make one aware and
sensitive to the mysteries that conditioned the person whose
existence you are acting."* End of entry.

The morning passed. Jacques had not yet been able to pee.
Now he was pacing back and forth on the grey carpet trying to
decode from the years of illicit entries on guardians, mysteries
and questions, some passage that would untangle the closing
of the events which now suspended his heart from weak and
empty strings in his hollow chest.

He sat down, stood up again, they pounded his fist hard on
the desk. He grimaced as the pain numbed his fist. Grains of
cocaine fell away from the final neat line. Gently he massaged
the pain with the other hand.

On the walls of the office surrounding his black desk hung
prints of paintings done by his grandfather. His eyes looked in
the direction of his favorite one that showed a man running

from a camera. The running man's legs, torso and arms were classically drawn, except for his head which was a long daub of purple and yellow paint.

He looked away from the painting and its flagrant conception, nagged by a smothered, but insistent, thought:

'You are dead by published report and you can step outside to confirm it.' Slowly, he extended the fingers of his hurting hand and tried to devise ways to verify his existence.

"Aha," he said. "I will call *The Times* and ask them to send over a reporter to bring me back into existence. He picked up the phone. There was no dial tone. Only a series of low clicks as when a phone is partially disconnected.

"Pisses me off," Jacques shouted. "Pisses me off! Imagine that the photo was actually put there, in the newspaper, on purpose. That my death is going to be destined and contrived by men as pompous as myself. But to what end? Am I to be killed because they are in pursuit of some event, some end, the results of which even they cannot predict for there is no end. All events continue into eternity."

She banged loudly on the front door, the only entrance from and exit to the street.

"Jacques, open up. I know you're in there." It was the voice of a woman.

Jacques kept silent, automatically holding his breath and listening intently. Then he said aloud, "Fuck it." He snorted the remaining white line.

It filled his being with a cool bravado. The pounding on the door continued. He jumped on his desk and pushed at the white fiberglass square of the lowered ceiling and barely caught the Uzi before the gun hit his face and he had to let himself be covered with dust from the old, weak newspapers and brown-yellow faded photographs that fell from the ceiling onto the desk covering the open diary. The Uzi was his weapon of choice resulting from an unimaginable act of Hitler and the Allies in the murder of six million Jews. With twisted logic, he was convinced that if you killed with the Uzi you helped to forgive God.

The pounding on the door stopped. Written on the open page of the diary now buried under the scattered heap of newspapers was this:

Do not believe that those who chose me as a guardian are aware of the mysteries I protect. They are not. They are usually the true believers in the definitions. They become angry and adamant when anyone tries to explain the mystery behind the definition. They especially believe their definitions of power. I graduated from training and was congratulated and told I would have the opportunity to decide the future history of individuals and nations. Bull. A successful socialist revolution occurred in Cuba separated from the American military base only by a cheap barbed wire. It is a joke. The mystery always overwhelms the limits of definitions. For mysteries contain all the other possible ways of making the definition. End of entry.

Jacques brushed the dust from his double-breasted leather suit. Then shook it from the newspapers and photographs. He was reaching among the newspapers for the diary when the face of his grandfather smiled up at him from one of the antique brown photographs. The smile was still, self-conscious and socially aware. A style of smiling that had been fashionable at the turn of the century. He noticed that he was now older than his grandfather was when the picture was taken. Again, he was made aware of his mortality, for some reason unknown to him, his anger subsided. He stacked the newspapers carefully, then sat down. He re-read the stories and looked at the old photographs. He read the old news intently, purposefully, and succeeded in closing from his mind the incessant hollow thoughts of his finality by establishing a backward continuity with his grandfather and an infinite and indecipherable past.

The hours passed, quick and tense, like the second hand on a large clock. His predicament rose again in his mind as he glanced at the time on his watch. He concluded that he was being sacrificed to win support for counter-insurgents in South America or to show that terrorists were operating in the city or for whatever reason. Christ! With an ungreased metallic gradualness he swallowed the acceptance of his finality. "Maybe I don't even exist. Maybe I am just a mass of learned responses."

With that thought, he got up and pushed the Uzi into the waist of his pants. Its presence made an effort to reassure him. It didn't. Jacques pulled his yellow leather overcoat with its overstated lapels onto his tall, slim frame. He knew he couldn't stay, hiding forever among portraits. He had to go. But where? Where didn't matter. Never mattered. As he walked toward the exit and the inevitable threat of the inevitable outdoors, he remembered the story Mr. Clark told him when he had confessed that he believed the liberation theology of rebel priests.

They were sitting on the crooked steps in front of a precariously built wooden shack that had served as their temporary headquarters for the Nicaraguan contras. Combat boots had bruised away the grass leaving a clearing of dusty brown earth around the shack. Beyond the clearing, the matted, green jungle surrounded them.   Mr. Clark was dressed in camouflage army fatigues, the green jungle reflecting in his spit-shined black boots. Jacques wore a loose-fitting blue T-shirt and khaki pants, his sandals hanging limp on his feet. The canvas bag that held his diary was slung over his shoulder.

Clark looked at him with a smile that did not suggest friendliness and said, "I'll tell you a story. God, who only has one eye, made man in his image. Thus he gave man one eye and a singular perception. The devil, a contradictory fellow who has many eyes, decided to play a trick on God. Laughing loudly, he gave man another eye and then, with an even louder laughter, he gave man two ears. From that day on, man has been searching for his one eye and singular perception.

On page 26 of the diary, Jacques had written:

"Here are the three possible alternatives. The soldier's final reduction of man to being and thinking. Cogito ergo sum! This is an appropriate predicate for man's attitude and achievement. And that of the false Egyptian prince, who

after crossing the desert, became a shepherd and then spoke to God, said that God made one more reduction when speaking himself. He said, 'I am the I am.' Thus, he described himself as only beingness. That forces the question. Was God upset with the shepherd because he destroyed the commandments, or for being angry at the idol worshippers? Which further asks the question, how could God be angry with the shepherd at all? Being pure beingness, he must feel equally sympathetic to both the shepherd and the idolaters.

Then there was the woodworker who disowned Joseph and claimed God for a father and described his beingness as pathway. This could only occur if the woodworker's definitions were always questions. A search for the eternal solution."

Jacques unbolted the door. Again the phone rang. Its bells startled him. His body coiled. A tingle of vibrations rushed up his spine. He picked up the receiver from the extension on the gallery wall next to the door.

"Hello."

"Hello, Jacques." Mr. Clark's voice sounded amused and close. "If you had taken the world of man seriously, then you would have had a chance of fate killing you mercifully at an unexpected moment, but ..."

Jacques let go of the receiver. It bumped against the wall and dangled from its cord.

He stepped quickly out of the gallery onto the street. His imagination placed a faceless man with a high-powered rifle somewhere behind one of the hundreds of windows that surrounded the street. He did not close the door behind him. There was a drizzle. He walked quickly. The entrance to the underground trains marked by the green light was ten yards away. The yards stretched out for hours. The afternoon skies were dark and burdened with rain. The air was heavy and mute. Every footstep he took was an act suspended in a long moment of self-awareness. In those moments he constantly checked on himself, making sure that he was still there. The streets were black and wet. The buildings, thick stark clusters of straight lines, rose from the earth. Their windows eyeballed him. Sounds of footsteps. Splashing water under the wheels of cars. Hooded knives and pistols. Innocent-looking murderers. He crossed the street on Broadway and Astor Place, tiptoeing on every moment. Ready to tighten and wince at the bite of the bullet. A metal square balanced on one of its edges.

He reached the entrance to the underground trains, ran down the stairs. Strong strips of black iron and a battered and stubborn turnstile separated him from the platform and access to the train. Hurriedly, he pushed a token into the slot on the turnstile and pushed against it. The turnstile creaked and spun. He walked onto the grimy, underground platform. The faces around him were unfamiliar and imposing. At each end of the platform the train tracks disappeared into dark and forbidding holes. A tall man wearing a long, black leather coat was standing at one end of the platform. His broad back and long black hair was turned to Jacques. Jacques tapped his side making sure the Uzi was still there. It was.

Out of the dark cavern came the train, a ragged metal worm. Its rubberless wheels squealing against the steel track. The train stopped. He got in. The door closed behind him. Not wanting the cramped position of sitting, he held onto the overhead strap and then looked at the faces in the car. The train lurched forward, squealed and began a steady raucous along its tracks. He crossed quickly into the connecting sub-way car. Instinctively, he looked behind him. The man in the long, black leather coat had followed him. Immediately he recognized Carlos, the Guatemalan rebel leader. The broad face, now heavily bearded, and the black hair extended to his shoulders.

He saw recognition quiver briefly in the thick mottled flesh that surrounded Carlos' small intense eyes, but then Carlos looked away with a relaxed and disinterested expression and leaned against the exit doors. Jacques stopped, walked back and leaned against the exit doors opposite to where Carlos stood. The train rumbled on.

Jacques scanned the bulky black jacket Carlos wore. Carlos glanced at Jacques quickly. Their eyes locked for a second. Jacques knew that they both knew that death was there also, along for the ride, and that he was the hunted.

Thus, being a man faced with the end of his beingness, Jacques began to think feverishly. To recall the entries of his diary, reaching into the mystery to define a solution.

The train was nearing the bridge. It would soon be crossing high above the Hudson River.

The thought of a dice game came to his mind. A game where at any time a roll of a six could be as important as the roll of a one or a zero, which occurs when the die lands cocked indecisively. What decided which roll was the important one?

Suddenly the solution to his plight was clear to him. He

was the tossed dice and if he could change himself he could affect the outcome of the roll. He could kill the blonde woman sitting next to him. The one reading the romance novel. He would also kill Carlos, but only out of necessity. He reasoned that such actions would make him a useless sacrifice. The agency would have to scrap their plans to kill him, since they could no longer claim him as the heroic agent slain in pursuit of freedom. He considered the act, thinking, "In a game of dice, all rolls are valid."

A lively clarity filled his head. He felt his balls hanging heavily between his legs behind a stout penis and the full steady beat of his heart in a strong stomach. He began to piss. The urine came automatically. It flowed out wet and warm on his leg, into his shoe and onto the hard, metal floor.

The train rumbled on. Carlos stood there. Jacques stood there. The dirty steel columns held up the street above. The train passed through the column. He would wait for an opportunity. What the agency called a 'dead spot'. When the train was screeching to a stop and the passengers began to rise from their seats. Then. He imagined himself rapidly reaching for and pulling the Uzi from his waist. He could hear the rhythm of exploding bullets shake his arm, vibrate his eardrum. He imagined the blonde's blue eyes widening and her right eye becoming a red hole as blood splattered the blonde hair.

The train rumbled on. Jacques stood there questioning the intended act. Between questioning and being, he was searching for other solutions.

The train emerged from the dark tunnels and onto the bridge. Drops of urine fell from the train into the waters below. The train lumbered on. Its weight was heavy on the bridge above the polluted waters.

part III - man at his best

TIME WAITS IN THE MIRROR

I am standing here at the night table, daubing my shaving brush back and forth, putting lather on my face. I will shave before I go to bed. The lather on my face looks like a wreath of white roses.

Tonight he did not look at me but asked why I shaved at night. He told me that if I shaved in the morning it would make me look fresh and brisk. I responded and now I stand here staring into the mirror locked in the dilemma of that response. I stare into the mirror and I can see him. The mirror hangs above the basin of water. The embers of bright expectation are reflected in his eyes. I will use the water to wash the soap from the heaviness under my eyes and the deepening lines of my face.

I stare at him and he stares at me. Look, he stands in the

mirror surrounded by walls covered with picture poster heroes and bound philosophical theses. He is turned in on himself and is angry with me. He grasps the camera. When it was bought for him years ago, he would not think of doing with it that which he now intends.

Tonight we are not friends. There is spite and malice between us. The back of the camera is removed and the film exposed to the light. Tonight we are like the razor and the hard stubbles of hair that crackles under the lather as I drag the razor along my cheeks.

I think of him and he thinks of me. He is thinking of me now. He is tense and holding the camera tightly in his hand. He is planning to smash it against the walls, out of spite and hatred for me.

I knew it would come to this. I didn't know it when I hit him. He had come to my room with questions and to complain of the scent of mothballs from the garden of wilting lilies. He stared at me when he asked, why don't I get rid of the soap dish and shaving brush that each night for twenty years I washed the soap from, and placed on the left side of the basin of water. He told me that now there were such things as electric razors.

Just look at him there in the mirror. There is a sprinkle of grey in the hair that is receding above a high forehead and his stomach is no longer hard and muscular. It has become soft and heavy under the leather jacket. So I smacked him. That was my response.

Maybe I shouldn't have but if I didn't he wouldn't be angry with me now. He wouldn't be pacing the room, cursing under his breath, holding the camera in front of him, ready to smash it.

Maybe I should not have hit him? If I didn't he would not experience the disdain and spite and compassion he is now feeling.

It is good that I hit him. I should have hit him harder, cursed him and chased him from my room.

I want him to be sullen and spiteful, to break the camera, to do something that's foolish and futile. Ha.

For if he does that I will know that he still needs me. I will feel meaningful and responsible. I will still have a commitment to him.

I am a liar. I don't know whether I would prefer him to keep the camera safe or break it. If he keeps it safe it will show he is mature. That action will provide him with his own space at an unreachable and sometimes smirking distance from me. If he breaks it, I can smirk and keep him with me.

So, I want him to break it then. I am getting old. My existence is beginning to blur. Soon I will be meaningless. My actions will annoy no-one. If I stand in the town square and piss on the flag, passersby will make excuses for me. They will say forgive him for he is only an old fool. If I shout at them and say, "I don't want to be excused, I hate the flag," my shrill, hoarse voice will fall on deaf ears. If I become sad, contrite and, with tears in my eyes, make excuses for myself by saying, "I am sorry, I don't know, but today I am not myself," they will look away before I am finished speaking.

And if I stand in the town square and block the midday traffic, drivers will get out of their cars, grab me by the arms and try to pull me to the sidewalk. I would resist, push my heels stubbornly against the street and, like a mule, hang my ass back and attempt to sit. This may anger them. A policeman dressed in black and wearing white gloves may come running out of nowhere, a whistle in his mouth. He may give me a firm kick in the ass. Then I would straighten up, walk quickly to the sidewalk while joyously rubbing my backside with a feeling of inner happiness. Yes, I would remove my false teeth, let my wrinkled cheeks fall soft about my lips and then I would smile broadly.

But as soon as I am out of the way, the drivers would return to their cars. The traffic will flow again and the policeman who kicked me would forget about me. Well.

Maybe my descent into that obscurity has already begun.
I will know tomorrow if I look around his room and find that
he has rested the camera down gently.

I want him not to break the camera, to begin walking
away from me, to go out into the world and grasp it firmly with
his own hand. He has all this time held my hand in his,
making his hand into a glove into which I pushed mine and
through which he arranged the world.

If he does not break the camera it means that all I can
teach is learned, and I can no longer trap him in the illusions
of anger and spite and forgiveness that I set for him. It will
also indicate that I have become meaningless.

What should I do? I can only wait and see. I am a man
with no control over the future of these events. I took the risk.
I hit him, albeit without knowing that I was taking a risk. I
was just being what I am and thus I have exposed myself to my
own obscurity.

Listen. I want to be meaningless. I want to sit in deserted
libraries dressed on summer days in shabby brown raincoats
and intermittently blow my nose and cough and spit phlegm
into soiled handkerchiefs. If there is anyone sitting nearby,
that will annoy them. They will glimpse at me in disgust,
shake their heads and ask themselves 'why can't he stop

clearing his throat? Why doesn't he wash that disgusting handkerchief?' And I'll cough again and spit.

After a while they will get up and move away. Let them go. I desire the obscurity of insignificance so that I can meditate on wreaths of white roses, cloak myself in the quiet of graveyards and mumble my way backwards through the murky images of my life.

But if he is still with me, still breaking cameras, I will be forced to be meaningful. To shy away from the morbid contemplations to which I secretly look forward. The contemplations of the mystery of the nothingness of death.

When I can sweetly and undisturbingly contemplate my finality and am able to let others make excuses for me he would be in his own time. He would have faded from me into an infinite and empty space.

After I finished shaving last night, I didn't wash the soap from the shaving brush. I threw it aside on the table. I couldn't sleep. My insomnia raged. Eventually in the early hours of the morning I fell asleep. When I awoke I looked into the mirror and there was a dark stubble shading my face.

On the night table was the camera. It had been smashed.

Now although the years have passed, and my hair is completely white, I look in the mirror and I can still see him.

Because of him, I sit in libraries wearing neat, blue blazers and I avoid coughing even though here is a scratching in my throat and the handkerchief hidden in my pocket is clean. I ignore my doctor's advice. I breathe deeply in the clean clear summer's air. I expect that on my deathbed the dilemma will return. For the time being, I wink at pretty girls. They walk by, and, over my shoulder, I briefly concern myself with the shape and motion of their posteriors.

I had not thought that it would be possible to break cameras while at the same time say goodbye.

SAGA QUARTS

They say things don't change on St. Cortez, but don't
worry, after one time is two time. Look at Saga Quarts now.
You see, I get old and lost the seine, and listen man, I never
one day thought 'bout Japanese or 'bout machines sucking out
sand from Lordstown harbour.

Is looking at me now sitting here on the sand, mending
somebody else fishing net, bent over wearing this straw hat,
shading sun from the eyes, that does make passersby
remember things like the night at the Boxing Day dance when
Police George started a fight with Saga Quarts. Police George
didn't know who he was playing with.

They say Police George run from Grenada and came to St.
Cortez. He married Miss Woods daughter, then turn

policeman. Them days Saga Quarts was a cocksure, short crotch seine-captain almost always dressed in a khaki short pants, with a cap pulled down over my eyes, which made me look like I had Chinese or Carib blood, and if anyone was brave enough and they wanted their ass cut they could come and call me, Fu Manchu.

Anyway, at the Boxing Day dance on the same night the fellow Ralph held the first public communist meeting in Lordstown Square, Saga Quarts was picking up tickets at the door of Queens Hall, I was dressed up like a sweet man, sweat on the forehead and wearing a red shirt and cream coloured long pants, with a red washrag flowing out of the back pocket oui, and the dollars I collected I spread out like a fan in my left hand. I was a show off, yes. All this time it was baccanal for so inside the sweaty, half dark, dance hall. The calypso music was blasting down the place and women and men, frantic, winding up and down their waists.

My partner Sweet Needle came to the door to catch some fresh breeze, and I was telling him the fast bowlers going to mash up England, when Police George dressed up like a sweet man himself walk up to me. I had one leg stretched out blocking the door, oui. Move your short crotch and let me pass, he say. Boy I just looked all the way up in this big, ugly, policeman's face. I say, pass where. He say, move. I going to inspect the dance.

The policeman must be think that because I is a fisherman I stupid too. Where you hear police does inspect dance. You have a ticket?

He answer with, man, ah say move your short ass. Why police so boasting, eh? And Police George up and push me.

Bad move. Saga Quarts raise up on his toes and slap Police George - bap. Then I back up, took off the white saga boy hat, slip the dollars in the sweat band and spin it over to the partner leaning by the door. Police George rush in with two big cuffs. I bobbed the cuffs and weaved to the side. Oui. Police George is a joker. He think because he big he can fight.

Right then, two more partners come to the door to cool off and chat. They see what was going on and only smile. They lean up 'gainst the door as cool as ever and cross one foot cross over the other, with their hands in their pocket, a toothpick hanging on one side of the mouth and cigarette on the other side.

Police George confident now that I just duck, swerve and ain't try to hit back, rushed in with a wild punch. This time I didn't move.

I heard a partner tell Pokeup put a ten dollar on Police George nuh, I going put a twenty on Saga Quarts? Pokeup say, I look stupid tonight, right?

I step inside the Police George punch, right inside he two big arms, right in he crebbie. Quick as ever, I hold him behind the neck and jumped, head bowed like a damn ram goat. Bap with the top of the forehead, right in Police George face. Then I jumped back before the blood spout and dirty up my sweet boy clothes, and I took the red washrag out my pocket and wipe the perspiration off my face.

Police George confused. He feel the blood on he face and started spinning like a fowl without a head on Christmas morning. Then Sweet Needle leaning on the door slowly take out his tooth pick. Tha' man had big lips, oui. He took a puff on the cigarette and walked over with the brim, put it on top me head and say. I got to crown you again boy. The other partner, Pokeup uncrossed his legs gave me a bow, and stroll back inside the dark, hot hall to take a dance. This time Police George done rush across the street and he only shouting. 'You better hide. I'll be back for you backside.'

And he did come back with a whole van of policemen.

But wait, I talking about how things change, boy. Things

was changing even back then you know. But in these small islands change always seem to come from the outside and the change don't stay, only change again, oui. Look at Flower Gardens where I renting a small room now. Saga Quarts did live there like a king on the north end of Lordstown in a two story limestone and shingle house. I bought that when I came back from sailing with National Bulk.

That's what ah saying. Poor people didn't always live in Flower Gardens. But look how things change when one English man Mr. Duck decided to start a banana industry on St. Cortez and England and America call out for migrant workers, people got unsettled and they left the island like schools of sprat, opening up space in Flower Gardens for country people to come to Lordstown to look for their futures. And meanwhile the townspeople who make the money, one way or other, from the banana company, up and moved to new houses on places like Lowland Hill where the same country people used to plant with dasheen and banana.

All this moving left only the old people in Flower Gardens and as they died their children cut up the big houses into hot little rooms and rent them out to the women who all the time pregnant with their naked brown children, and all the time hungry, and yelling, playing, screaming, crying, and holding onto the frocktails of worn out, cheap print dresses of the mothers who live in the little rooms with the woodlice partitions plastered with colour pictures of gourmet food and movie stars. That's when Flower Gardens changed and I became the boss man amidst the wild growing lean-to shacks of rusty galvanized and saltfish box board, narrow alleyways, lumps of children tutu, and muscular listless men, with dreadlocks that grow like jungles all over Flower Gardens and all kinds of shacks was put up on every unowned patch of land.

But is just yesterday I was sitting here on the sand and a partner tell me that, the Banana Company planning to leave St. Cortez and I hear England and America going to stop immigration, so change going to come again. That must be why the police did raid Ralph the communist home Wednesday night just before the day turn morning.

But Saga Quarts didn't think 'bout the changes. I used to sit in the big seine boat on the blue waters of Lordstown Harbour waiting for the small fry to come into the harbour and the big fish to come after them to feed and splash 'bout in the water so I could throw the seine 'round them.

That's why Police George was so stupid. Wait, I going to tell you what happen with him. But look man, on the days when the seine catch plenty fish, you should see me, dressed in khaki short pants, my sun turn, dark red brown, copper skin, tight with muscles. I used to jump and stand on the bow of the boat full of fish and sea water, my short legs stretch from one side of the boat to the other, selling fish, my fist and the pocket of the khaki short pants full with money. That alone was enough to make them women of Flower Garden love me.

And them times Saga Quarts eyes look more Chinese and I walking 'bout Flower Garden patch up streets as though current flowing up in me from the earth. Yes man, I had women for so, and children; don't talk 'bout children. Every way you turn is one of Saga Quarts picknie and it seem the more children I made, the more women I get. You don't have to be a priest to figure out why. I could tell you, every woman like a nice dress to wear and a new shoe for she foot and food for she child, and the women them living in Flower Gardens poor, but nice looking with big backside and no education and no work and even if they get work by Samuel Store or at Tennison's, or as a servant girl, is only 'bout ten dollars a week they does pay them.

And it ain't only the poor girl and them I could get you know. If I did only start wearing long pants and build a house in Valsie Beach, I could rooster the high class women. For the women them with their husband working as civil servant for three hundred dollars a month, even though they fresh like bushbug can't resist an aggressive rooster like me on the run with a red washrag flowing from the back pocket and a fist full of dollars. You think I dreaming, right?

Going back to Police George, any bet if it was Baldwin or even Mr. Henry the postman standing by the door of the dance picking up tickets Police George would have some respect and manners, but no is me, Saga Quarts so he feel he could mash me down and step over me.

The police man might be bright but he stupid. He didn't know that Saga Quarts was the boss man of Flower Gardens and you could say I had my own army. Now look I have the men who does row the seine boat. Them men strong. They make jail already. Them men drinking all that fresh fish broth and rowing them big backside oar. And wait, we ain't even count all the men on the beach who does pull in the net for a handful of fish and the loud, cuss mouth women and them who does pull seine too, or who does buy fish from he to sell in the market. When them woman open up their cuss mouth on you, Oh Jesus Christ! Lord, Is murder! Plus all the boy children I have big and small with the same dirty mouth women and don't count the drunkards who always begging me for a drink of strong rum. I was a king in Flower Gardens and ain't 'fraid jail. I still respect the policeman alright, but like one bad dog respect the other.

Putting all that aside if Police George had come by the door and say, Saga Quarts boy, I going take a fete you know; or you know how policeman salary low, let me in nuh.

Saga Quarts would have take down his foot and let him in. I would even send one of the boys with him to the bar and buy a couple of beer for him. But no! Police George want to play bad.

Ten minutes after he run off bleeding a vanload of about a dozen policemen came speeding and burning brakes, pulling up and jumping out before the van stopped; rushing toward Saga Quarts with hats pushed back on their foreheads, long riot batons, and big buckle leather belts 'round their waists, with that bragging bull dog Sargeant Truck leading them, swinging a nice, short baton ready to burst man head. Police George was walking alongside him like a she-she, still holding the handkerchief on his face like a damn little boy. Them thing does vex me you know. What's the problem here Saga Quarts? Sargeant Truck say.

I tell him, well the Grenadian boy there want to come in the fete, so I ask him if he have a ticket. The man up and try to cuff me down.

Is that so ? Truck said, turning to Police George. Well, Sir, he wouldn't let me in the dance.

Sargeant Truck suck his teeth. George is that why you want to beat Saga Quarts. Get in the van and let's go.

Somebody should have let the Police George know that Truck and I is second cousin and that all Cortezians related somehow. No big foot Grenadian policeman was going to come here and beat me.

But Police George still ain't satisfied yet, so he organized two other stupid big foot policemen from out Gomea and come out now into the heart of Flower Gardens to start trouble, oui.

I was in Miss Hewitt rum shop dressed in my short khaki pants, drinking a Guinness stout and talking about how the damn rain won't stop for the cricket to play and let the West Indians mash up the Englishmen at Lords. Right then the policemen stepped in the rum shop.

I had my back turn but I hear Boyce the drunkard tell Police George, what the hell you'll want in here. Police George say Hush your damn mouth before I put this big black boots in it. I turned. Drunken Boyce was leaning on the drum of kerosene and Police George was watching him with bad eye.

Quick as ever, Saga Quarts spin off his hat and man,

Police George lift up he baton. He say, you just raise that damn head. Ah go bust it today though.

He talk too quick, My oldest boy, Braggart walk in the shop, same time. The boy tall like a coconut tree and he have a temper like a hurricane. Blows start to pelt, two head get bust, and the big foot policeman them run like fugitive out the rum shop, and up Harbour Street and is bottle and stone bursting behind them.

Then it was a stand off. Saga Quarts and the partners went in the seine boat and row out in the blue waters of Lordstown harbour. The police boat was leaking so Saga Quarts and the fellows just relaxed and waited for fish to start feeding and splashing about. A van load of policemen came down Flower Garden and waited on the beach. Later I hear somebody say that Sargeant Truck clout Police George and ask him, boy why you so? Why you like to start trouble so? And Police George say, No sir. Is not me sir. Is the drunkard Boyce who start it. He was leaning on the kerosene drum when I walk in the shop and asked me what the hell I want.

So guess what, they lock up Boyce and cut his ass well, wet him down with a fire hose and throw piss on him in the cell for starting the trouble.

Then Sargeant Truck came to the beach and waved to me

and I waved back sitting in the big seine-boat looking over Lordstown blue harbour and thinking how the waters large and blue and full with fish, not seeing or knowing 'bout Japanese trawlers that were just outside the harbour, catching the fish before they come into the harbour close enough to the shore for me to throw the net 'round them. Boy I tell you after one time is two time.

Later that year Prime Minister Marcus beg the Canadian money and started dredging Lordstown harbour to build a deep water wharf. So the fish stop coming near the shores. The water get too deep for the fish and for the seine. The next year I had to sell his seine.

Well that was that, the women and them gone you know? And they say that because the fellow Ralph started the communist party, nice God fearing foreigners sent the government a new patrol boat, machine guns and explosives for a special defence force, and is now the police them get arrogant for so. They make me glad I get old now because I would punch one of them right in their mouth, yes.

You see things does change on St. Cortez you know, but from the outside.

THE LEGEND OF JOME

It is said that this the legend of Jome was told by Columbus in the year of our Lord 1492 on an island which he left nameless on which numerous skeletons were found. The island we shall here call the Isle of Horror since it marks the time and place from which commenced the centuries of the beast.

Columbus was standing on the beach of the island. Anchored next to the shore was a rowboat. Further out in the harbor were the Pinta, the Nina and the Santa Maria. In the rowboat was a Carib. He was tied to the oars and except for a red burn on his chest - a branded insigna of the Spanish crown - his skin was copper, his hair long, black, his eyes had an oriental cast. He looked inwards with a despondent mood of self loathing, a sad anger turned his lips down. The twilight was blue on the white beach and the surf was quiet on the shore. Columbus self proclaimed messenger of god in search of the mongol Khan, stood on the beach, looked out at the Caribbean sea and theorized that the world was shaped like a woman's breast. He looked past the native in the boat and thought that the man was looking at him with a malignant stare. A fly buzzed Columbus' nose.

On the beach behind him, one thousand four hundred and ninety two Caribs had been made to kneel in the sand. Their bodies formed a brown square. Their wrists, like the oarman's were tied, but behind their backs and then to their ankles and then to each other. Four pale men stood with broad swords unsheathed stood at the cardinal points of the anguished square. The fly landed on Columbus' sweaty forehead. He slapped at it. It buzzed past his ear. He reached behind him and scratched the crack of his backside. "Remember the Moors," he shouted.

The pale men hacked their way through the bound and kneeling men, cutting a bloody cross of dead men until they met each other at its center and holding their bloody swords aloft they shouted "for God and country." Then they slaughtered with crazed abandon. "They worship a murdered god," said one of the kneeling men. "They believe their god died for their good. Therefore they can murder in its name."

A scream from the far side of the bloody square. A child tried to stand and run. The others died silently and when the last Carib was murdered, the red sun had sunk one inch behind the sea and the pale full moon made a sheen on the coral sand and the sand glistened with blood. Crabs scurried over the grassy red sand.

Crushing leaves of fake cinnamon and sniffing Columbus barefooted, cross eyed and clad in white rumpled trousers summoned the murderers to him.

"Cut off a thousand hands for pickling in the barrels and keep your bloody clothes, for they would guarantee us access to Queen Isabella's court."

Columbus climbed into the rowboat. Three others climbed in after him. The last man aboard pulled the anchor from the dark waters.

"Row."

The despondent Carib oarsman splashed the oars in the water. He rowed toward the three ships through a twilight that was heavy with his grief. The boat moved over the water toward the anchored ship. The ship loomed closer. The Caribstared at Columbus but did not see him. He thought of the dire and unknown fate that he knew awaited him and contemplated suicide.

Columbus sniffed the leaves. In the light of the pale moon. The steady stare of the oarsman annoyed him. The oarsman saw the annoyance in the rows of wrinkles along Columbus' brow and now stared at him deeply. The fly buzzed Columbus' head.

He reached for his dagger. The fly landed on his hand. He unsheathed the dagger and moved toward the native. The boat was unsteady in the water. The native did not shift his stare. Columbus lunged with the dagger. The fly jumped from Columbus' hand. The dagger punctured the oarsman's skin, the pressure of a hand grabbed Columbus' wrist, its knuckles white and tense.

"You shan't kill him. He is no longer a man. He is property. The property of the Spanish crown."

Columbus looked at the native, saw the red burnt wound on his chest, the insignia of the Spanish crown.

The buzz passed his ear again. The black fly hung in the dark sky. Columbus stabbed at it. The oarsman's stare was now broken by intermittent glances of longing at the corpses on the receding shore. Gradually Columbus allowed himself to face the constant accusation in the oarsman's eyes.

"I think he wants to know, would my god on the cross allow you to murder his people?"

Columbus answered in a language the oarsman did not understand to a question he did not ask.

Our god would permit it, but ours is not the god of the cross. I am god's hand on earth and I have thought of this on the windless days. I know now that it is not the god of the cross that guided our tense stomachs over the desert of the ocean.

Our god is, let's give him a name, call him Jome. He lived as a man among a nomadic tribe of my ancestors. Then they were outcasts, lesser children of the gods living in the lands of ice. They crossed rivers and mountains, roamed with animals, drank their milk, and blood, slaughtered them for food, staying alive, only one step ahead of a killing season, the white cold of winter, that you, my naked slave blessed with these warm lands know nothing of; an iron cold that locks the sky and makes the earth as hard as stone.

On an autumn day the tribe came to a river where the water rushed wild and white against the rocks. They set up camp for the night and Jome walked to the river bank. He stood alone at the river's edge and spoke with himself saying, 'I have crossed many rivers but when I am old and my bones are soft and brittle, a river such as this will bend my knees, break my bones and drag me under. Or maybe knowing I was about to die, I'd beg my companions to help me cross that river. Maybe on that day they would help me but one day they will leave me behind and I will bade them farewell before I starve to death on this side of my last river.'

Jome walked back to the camp, stood at its edge and with his big toe he drew a line in the dirt and shouted. 'This line is my last river. I dare anyone to cross it.'

Men and women came out of their tents and gathered around on the other side of the line. They looked at the broad shouldered towering unkempt figure of Jome with his long blond and greying beard. They remembered his capacity for cunning and violence and the fact that he could eat two wild pigs for one meal. They stood there, smiled at him and chatted with each other but none crossed the line in the dirt. And then nudged forward a laughing man crossed it. As he stepped past, he was knocked cold by Jome's thick fist. The men of the camp laughed and one after the other until nightfall they tried to cross Jome's last river.

The four sailors in the rowboat listened closely to Columbus.

The native oarsman rowed slowly. Neither the sailors nor Columbus knew how longingly he looked at the dark water nor that his toes twitched.

Columbus continued, "None crossed; with force and guile he defeated even the strongest. On that night, Jome built his tent on the side of the line he claimed as his own but he was unable to become blank and vanish into the infinity of sleep. The scent of his death emerged from where he kept it tucked away in the obscure future that now loomed in front of him, dark against his face. Tortured by its possibilities, he stumbled about the sleeping camp. Returning to his tent he lay down, and stared at the darkness that rested on his eyeballs. His body felt every bump of the uneven crust of the earth under the spread of his blanket of animal skin. His thoughts were focused on his last river.

That next morning at dawn when the men were preparing for the crossing, Jome stepped out of his tent obsessed and delirious with the incredible idea that despite all the land that stretched out in front and behind him as far as the eye could see - he shouted to the camp he owned the land on the other side of the line on which his tent was pitched and the twelve goats he had pulled to that sides.

The headman shouted, 'C'mon Jome stop the madness. We need your help to cross the river.'

'No I am not crossing the river. This is my land and the goats on it are mine also.'

Everyone laughed. The headman said, 'Don't be stupid, the earth stretched forever, we walk it for forty, fifty seasons and then we pass into the sky.'

Jome deepened the line with his toe. This time he un - sheathed his dagger.

The eyes of the tribe turned to the headman. He walked to Jome smiling. He was about to put his arm around Jome's, when Jome stabbed him in the heart.

The people looked at him aghast. Several rushed to fetch Orsu the headman's son. Twelve men led by Orsu came back with blades drawn and they say only the retreating figure of Jome running among the boulders on the hill chasing a dozen goats ahead of him.

They rushed after him, pebbles scattering downhill under their sandals. At nightfall they returned without him. He had vanished they said, with his animals among the caves and boulders of the hill.

That night Orsu and the twelve men slept beyond the line drawn by Jome. The next morning the women wailed. During the night their throats were slit.

The days passed. Each day a group of men went into the hills searching for Jome. The tribe remained camped at the shore of the river. None found him. Yet anyone who slept on the land claimed by Jome was murdered at night.

The men of the tribe became more determined to stay and murder him. The women agreed. The children had no choice and gradually the autumn ended. It was now too late to travel south to the warmer lands and the tribe moved into caves on the other side of the hill. They swore as the cold bit them, to murder Jome, convinced that hunger and the freezing weather would force him from the hills.

The winter was a horrible one. The goats that weren't slaughtered barely survived by scratching away the snow and eating the frozen grass below it and no one dared to go to the hillside Jome had claimed.

It was in the long nights of that winter, the legend of Jome began. Though no one said it then, in that winter of suffering, that winter of fights and murders over food and ownership of blankets or for looking at someone else a second too long, that winter convinced many of the tribe that maybe Jome was correct for by the coming the next spring, men had claimed women as their own, The remaining goats were divided. The women did not even have to withdraw their favors to convince their lovers to claim land for themselves the way Jome did.

When the summer came, the fruitless hunts to murder Jome continued. But the searches were carried out without passion even though two lovers who had slept beyond the line drawn by Jome were murdered. The unspoken fact was the people realized that they no longer had to cross turbulent rivers or dangerous mountain passes. Gradually rumors began to circulate that Jome was not a man but a powerful spirit. A shrine was built on the hill where he vanished and before every winter twelve goats were sacrificed to him.

The people realized also that they like most, wanted to be at peace in one place but everything else forced them to move, everything, even time moved them to their graves.

They were better prepared for the next winter, more survived and there were less murders. That spring wild plants that bore fruit were planted in the valley next to the river. A village grew there and then a city. Jome's teachings were written down and studied by all. Children learned to draw lines in the dirt and to fight anyone who crossed it.

The sailors cheered as Columbus finished his tale.

Suddenly the oarsman rushed to the side of the boat. The boat rocked. Columbus grabbed its sides . The sea rushed into the boat. The oarsman jumped. The dark waters covered him. He struggled with the large oars tied to his wrist. The last bubble of his breath burst on the surface.

'Get the oars,' Columbus shouted.

Two men dived overboard. Columbus spoke louder.

We are still nomads. For being in one place exhausts the land, the rules, exhausts the morality. In Jome's valley the strong and the cunning united and gradually seized the land and the goats of the weak and the stupid, and usurped their life force and usurped their time on earth and the labour of their strength. Ways of doing this were added to the teachings of Jome.

People were forced to leave the valley to find and steal and bring back whatever they could. And so it remains the strong continue to hoard and the adventurers continue to go forth and rob.

One day a man of the village brought back a cross with the figure of a man murdered on it, 'for our good' he said, and added that the murdered man was god's messenger and his message was that no one had to leave the village anymore for the god on the cross had devised a way so that everyone could live in peace. It was simple, everyone had to treat everyone else as they would like to be treated.

"I guarantee," Columbus said, almost to himself. "There will be others who will try to teach us how not to be nomads. But Jome lives in our hearts and stomachs. It was he that guided us over the waves." And so began the centuries of the rivers of blood.

CRIMSON BLOODED MEN

The attack on the barracks came early in the morning just as the stars began to vanish from the night's sky. Bernard Montalgar - a revolutionary with one wooden leg and the ambition to live forever led the attack balancing with precarious certainty above his peg leg, a steady darkness covering his face, a pistol in his pocket.

Ahead of him, in front of the barracks Constable Truck, the lone sentry on duty slowly paced back and forth in a night of blurred objects.

Constable Truck was tired. He could feel the weight of his bones sagging in his body and the hard rifle on his shoulder. The thick green foliage of the tropical night was wrung with a wet heat. It locked the sweating collar of his tunic to his neck. There was someone coming toward him, walking under the dark arches of the buildings. He heard the hollow clack of a wooden leg, a short pause, and then the hollow clack again.

He noted sleepily that the half wooden footsteps had an urgent rhythm.

There was something familiar about it, something abstract and theoretical. He tried to remember. He was too old for sentry duty. He was tired. He couldn't remember. He ignored the wooden footsteps.

Under his black pants of British flannel there was sweat on his legs and there were images in his fogged brain that his pants were made of a dense accumulation of insects glued together by a hot, damp sweat. The insects scurried about amid the black hairs and beads of sweat on his thighs and using sharp small mouths, they wiggled their way under his skin. He bent forward, began to scratch and peered into the blackness of the arches. He saw no one.

Anyway, he had heard the hollow clack of that wooden leg before; and now the world was becoming fogged and distant. Slowly and persistently his heavy eyelids were dragging his weary head downward. Soon he would begin to see murky pictures of his thoughts.

'Whose footsteps was it again?'

In the dark field that filled the space in front of his closed eyes he could see a transparent bubble. It formed out of the hollow sound of the wooden leg on the flagstone sidewalk. As the footsteps faded, the bubble expanded until it disappeared into nothingness. Then once again as the wooden leg hit against the flagstone he saw another bubble forming. Suddenly, unexpectedly, a hand reached out of the bubble and slapped his face. "Wake up."

His head jerked upward. His eyes opened. He shook his head and re-established a partial sense of himself behind slack and bulky eyelids.

Yawning, he looked about and realized that the clack of the wooden leg was now closer. Constable Truck peered into the darkness. Still no-one. He rested the heavy rifle against the pale brown and red stones of the barracks. The barracks was an old, imposing rectangular structure. Only the flagstone sidewalk and a narrow stretch of black pitch called Harbour Street separated it from the beach and the calm dark waters of the Lordstown Harbour. The barracks had been build by the British to protect the then colony from French imperialism.

Over the years the building kept its arrogance. Now it looked out to sea with the same boastfulness of the policemen who inhabited it.

Constable Truck loosened the sweating collar of his tunic. He decided that he would lean against the barracks, not sleep, only rest his heavy bones for a short while. For a month now he had been careful not to sleep. He was convinced that if he made another error the General would shoot him.

Two months ago when he was Commissioner Truck, Chief of Police he had shot and killed one of the police dogs after mistaking it for a man with crimson blood. A month ago he thought that he would never be suspected of having crimson blood; now he was not sure. Anyway, what crimson blooded men?

Again the weight of his eyelids began dragging at his weary head. He knew that he had been bogged down in a slow battle with sleep. A battle that he was determined to win even now that his eyelids were pasted over with a thick brittle glue and he completely missed the moment that he fell asleep.

There it was again, that transparent bubble, expanding with each hollow echo of the leg now distant far away, far away.

The bubble began to envelop him. He found himself in the domed interior of the echo. Inside it and he saw that its thin vaporous walls were not transparent. A dark blur of restless, half-formed images covered its bent screen.

Soon an unsteady image began to take shape. He recognized it as that of the dead youth lying face up on the cold, uneven floor of the prison cell and recalled that this was how it had all started and now the tense packed bricks of his fear shaped the dark image and the cell walls.

Even in the disordered ramble, of consciousness obstructed by sleep, he tried not to blame himself for the young man's death.

"Constable Truck, is you that did put blows on the fellow."

"But I was not the only one who had put a few blows on the youth."

"You pissed in his nose."

"So I was drunk. So he was a crimson blooded man I had a right ... how could that stifle him? ... so and anyway again you were ... drunk and anyway and anyway again , you ..."

"He didn't move when I pissed in his nose."

The thin bubble of his dream was continuously expanding. It was now as wide as a night's sky, elongating the immense image of the corpse on its thin and vacuous surface. With an expression of vacant solitude the corpse's face became a flat and ominous shadow then it changed into an old woman with a sad and frightened face. The old woman held tightly to the hand of a child. The child was laughing and excitedly trying to pull his hand away. The old woman faded and changed into the General. The General breathed deeply the faint smell of the corpse and he began to grow until he became a giant dwarf with short, stubby, muscular hands and legs. The medals covering the general's chest and stomach smelled like flowers at a funeral.

Truck was now transfixed in the reality of the murky dream.

Gradually the bubble expanded into nothingness and his self awareness dispersed in a moment of undisturbed sleep.

Montalgar, tall and black above the peg leg was now closer to the sleeping sentry. The jolting half wooden rhythm of his forward stride animated his banana-stained khaki shirt. The shirt flapped about in front of his stomach and chest. His wooden leg hit the pavement again, evoking Constable Truck back from the infinity of sleep, forcing him upward into the storehouse of dreams. Again the image of the bubble formed. On the sides of the bubble, around the expanding corpse of the young man who was accused of having crimson blood, were shadowy figures carrying the flames of hundreds of flickering candles.

Truck felt again the disgust that these people whom he protected would dare hold a candlelight vigil in front of the barracks to protest the death of a common criminal.

But now he saw his own outline wavering among the shocked shadows of ordinary people and the outrage of the

candlelight against the dark background of a once tranquil
island of ordinary people who knew each other.

As the sound of the leg faded and the bubble expanded the
image of the corpse and the angry fervor of the shadow
marchers created a dense mood that folded into the darkening
and stormy background of the ever expanding echo, leaving
only the bare and silent candle flames that became
increasingly miniaturized against the dark background. The
Constable's stomach was twisted with the tension of the dark
and clashing colors that painted the mood of the dream. The
memory that vomited the images of the dream was not of the
days of the candle light march but of the then unseen and
barbarous events that were yet to transpire.

That day after the demonstration, the Prime Minister,
now General, went on national T.V. Constable Truck, then
Chief-of-Police, was told to stand next to him as he made his
speech and was given an extra line of medals to wear.

The Prime Minister read from the tele-prompter. He had
fair skin and his eyes were crossed and bold. The right eye
looked toward heaven and the left eye looked at a non-existent
object. As always, his crossed eyes confused the viewers. It
made them feel as though they were out of focus.

He stammered throughout his speech. First he praised

God and then nationalism. Then he accused the young man who had been beaten to death of being a threat. He was a threat, the Prime Minister said, because he had crimson blood. He accused the opposition party for trying to stir up trouble. The speech dragged on and ended with him reminding the citizens to vote for him and his People's Progressive Party, since only they knew how to rid the country of these evil crimson blooded persons who lurked among the red blooded populace.

Montalgar who was now closing in on the sentry had listened sitting in a living room that was filled with the bareness of its walls. He heard the Prime Minister's speech amid the sounds of his common-law wife sweeping the kitchen. Before the speech was finished he had dismissed it with a downward slash of the hand and the thought that politicians had now progressed to insulting the ignorance of the people.

With both arms, he pushed his body up from the chair until he stood on his straight wooden leg, then he stomped toward the kitchen and tried to direct his thoughts to the excitement of the soccer game that was to be televised later. His mind returned to the speech. Something about it, something tight and undefinable had lodged in his stomach and daubed his chest, light and vaporous like rubbing alcohol.

On his way to the kitchen he let his thoughts ruminate over what could be significant about the speech other than it being ludicrous. He shrugged. He had other things to worry about.

Even though it was twenty years ago during the sugar riots that he had lost his leg - shot by Constable Truck who had been his childhood friend - Montalgar did not appear to have aged a day. His wide, handsome, black face still had a bold suddenness about it and his actions were still impulsive responding to the excitement of odd moments.

But the day of the speech was the second anniversary of his fortieth birthday. The birthday when he had discovered while shaving that he had lost his sense of urgency and had acquired a remarkable gift for rationalizing away whatever he wished.

It worsened on the following Monday. He awoke and was not able to give priority to any of his plans. It was then that it dawned on him that the angels were gradually preparing him for death.

He became determined to devise a scheme to disrupt their preparations and live forever. He considered the schemes of other men which sometimes consisted of not eating pork and singing slow songs in a church on Sunday mornings. He dismissed those schemes since they usually required that one die before beginning to live forever. Thus he devised a superior plan to stay alive which consisted of reading suspense novels, not saying his prayers, and eating green mangoes.

The speech had caused concern and an unconscious fear among the populace for up until then they thought they knew that crimson and red were the same color. Almost automatically, attendance dropped off at public political meetings of the Prime Minister's party. The Prime Minister realizing that his scheme had backfired decided that only propoganda could differentiate between crimson and red. To this end, he grew a beard, dressed in khakis and gave three hour speeches that decried crimson and praised red. At every street corner, he ordered the installment of giant billboards with red painted on one side and crimson on another. The campaign worked, for gradually the accusation against the youth was accepted and the outrage at his death subsided.

The only indication that the populace sensed that something off-center was afoot came on Sunday exactly one week and a day after the last billboard was put up. That Saturday night a thousand Cortezians including Montalgar dreamt that a nuclear bomb had been dropped directly on the roof of their houses. From August to December of that year, the sentry, then Police Chief, was surprised that in front of all the police stations he visited, people had formed long lines.

At the Complaints Desks, women reported that they had been raped by crimson blooded intruders. Bald men reported that their hair fell out after merely looking at the color. Children reported that they knew they had not finished eating supper but somehow the food vanished from their plates. Several persons reported that while combing their hair, the combs were stolen and then secretly put back among the folds of their hair. Men reported that they were awoken in the night by strange noises and found their wives murdered by crimson blooded intruders who then forced them to do abominable things to their daughters. An old woman holding two lost white chickens appeared at the barracks everyday.

Two days before Christmas, four diabetics accused Moses of causing the deaths of all the people buried in the Methodist church yard.

The Prime Minister instructed the Chief to increase the staff at the Complaints Desks, confident that if the frenzy of complaints kept up he had the elections won.

A change in events came when one week before elections, a crate containing guns, bibles and dollars arrived on the island. The crate was addressed to the Prime Minister. It came from a source that preferred not to be named but which promised more aid and expertise in identifying and wiping out crimson blooded persons.

The Prime Minister examined the contents of the crate and was flabergasted thinking that he must have stumbled on an International Society for the Creation of Enemies. He had merely wished to unleash a bit of the fear that each person carries their chest; a simple strategy to win the elections.

That night he analysed the possibilities inherent in the offer and devised grandiose plans whereby the murder of crimson-blooded people could become a national industry. That way he surmised he could kill two birds with one stone. Scuttle those he disliked and develop the economy. On that very morning he forged into existence a force of special constables whose task it was to go on early morning patrols in search of crimson blooded people.

It was then that the now sleeping sentry, then Chief-of-Police, shot a police dog after mistaking it for a crimson blooded man, the incident made headlines in the St. Cortez Herald and Prime Minister called Chief Truck to his office.

When Chief Truck entered the new oak-paneled, green carpeted office, the Prime Minister looked up, grunted, looked back down and continued writing. The minutes passed. The

Chief stood waiting. The air between them thickened.

"Have a seat."

Finally Chief Truck sat on the brown leather couch to the left of the Prime Minister's new mahogany desk. A painting of the English King dressed in medals and a purple sash stared firmly down at him. The chief removed his hat and adjusted his tie.

The Prime Minister looked up but because of his bold cross-eyed stare, the chief wasn't quite sure that he was looking at him; so to avoid being confused, he looked away toward the flag in the corner of the room.

"Constable Truck."

The Chief looked at the Prime Minister.

"I am disappointed. You have taken a threat to national security and made it into a joke."

"Sir, the error was a genuine one."

"Genuine?"

"Yes sir, it was dark and I mistook the dog for a crimson blooded man crawling toward me."

The Prime Minister spun around in his chair turning his back to the Chief.

And so after ten years as Commissioner, Chief Truck was stripped of his rank and given sentry duty. A new

Commissioner was appointed, placed in charge of the special forces and given one week to find a man with crimson blood.

He didn't have to look far. The next day an angry mob turned in a perplexed man whom they accused of having crimson blood. Again the island became tense with the undefined threat. The Prime Minister declared martial law and suspended elections indefinitely.

A week later, a plane load of explosives arrived on the island. That night during a nationally televised speech, the Prime Minister defined culture as the ability to put everything in its proper place and praised advanced culture for the ability to produce explosives that would kill only those with crimson blood.

Two days later he gave himself the title of General and Viceroy. Almost overnight, the sight of the sparkling Caribbean sea changed, and began to evoke a sense of thick, blue nausea, as the citizens increasingly realized that they were all suspect and that their world had flattened into two horrifying dimensions. One space was filled by special constables with eyes as blunt as hammers who choked a forced silence. The other dimension, the space over their shoulders, the place of departure was forbidden by law.

This absurdity angered Montalgar, bringing to the surface

a sense of his unrealized greatness activated by a 'cross-eyed clown'. And even now it boiled in his stomach as he moved on Constable Truck, hidden by the darkness of the arches, his fist wrapped around the cold metal of the gun.

On the beach about twenty yards from the barracks, four fellow conspirators, young and overburdened with themselves, knelt in the sand behind a red boat and awaited Montalgar's signal to storm the barracks.

The boat smelled of fish and salt water. The young men were tense. Peering over the side of the boat they kept an eye on the barracks and the sleeping sentry.

One of them whispered, "This is an omen of victory."

The other three nodded. Each was armed with homemade knives. The steel blades were slack in the wooden handles. Now under the pale moon they saw their leader approach the sleeping sentry.

"Get ready."

One of the men breathed in short rasps. Their agitated hearts dried up the saliva in their mouths. The smell of the fishing boat became stifling. They breathed harder.

Montalgar, tall and black above the peg leg, closed in on the sleeping sentry who remained transfixed in the reality of the murky dream images, totally oblivious to the reality of the

sound of the wooden leg. It was quiet in the early morning darkness, and except for the smell of the ocean and the gentle wash of the surf. The street stretched out black in front of him and Montalgar walked with himself and the dire implications of what he was about to do, thinking - 'Soon the fake general will know how absurd it is to cage
men without first feeding them with philosophy and dreams.'

Montalgar was now parallel to where Constable Truck slept and he heard the croaking resonance of the his snore.

He kept walking and out of the corner of his eye looked nonchantly at the Constable Truck, then he walked past him, stopped and turned.

Yes, the sentry was asleep and it was the ex-Police Commissioner Truck. The totally same man who had shot him in the leg during the sugar riots twenty years ago. A sweet and vile anger filled Montalgar.

He used to laugh long and loud when after the shooting of the dog the Chief became the butt of jokes. When it was said that he was born on the thirty-first of February, and that at the scene of a crime, the Chief had taken the front toe-prints of a pussy cat which he later submitted into evidence.

Contrary to expectation, these jokes had not humbled the Chief. Instead he adopted a regal bearing and increasingly became known for his brutality. When Montalgar realized this, the laughter no longer gave him pleasure or release. And now looking at Constable Truck, his mouth tasted of an arid hatred and he whispered silently.

"From this night on after I blow your bastard head off I will laugh not more when I hear the jokes, instead I will say to myself, the tiny lump of shit and then spit."

Montalgar stared intently at Constable Truck's face, noticing that the old mouth was hung open and dribble ran down the side of his grey lower lips. He noticed also how amazingly worn and innocent the round face looked except for a pair of nostrils that flared big and black inside, like the muzzle of a gun. But there were grey hairs straightened by mucus in the nostrils. It amazed him how frail and sinless the face was now that it was asleep and free of the pressure of having to put on appearances. And he realized that the old fellow's loud and vulgar snores were not meant for public ears. That the sleeping face was a private one meant only for Constable Truck's wife and children to see when the false teeth were removed and placed in a clean glass filled with water on the night table next to his bed.

"I'll kill the bastard anyway."

But the anger in Montalgar did not rage anymore. Now

that he was standing in that shifting and dire space where the possibilities for momentous and absurd futures converged. He was absorbed by the nature of that unforgiving void which would open the moment the act was done. To fail meant certain violent death, to succeed meant the Presidency, a rage of parades and speeches with him as the center of attention, the power to change the flag, to take political prisoners, to exchange murder for aid, and also to lay awake at night in fear of the next coup.

Between these two possibilities were the ghostly outlines of countless futures, all equally dreadful.

The sleeping of Constable Truck allowed him to hover there in the turmoil of indecision. He could still walk away and continue the existense of an ordinary man which was much worst, since he now knew of his own unrealized greatness. Yet whether he succeeded or not, the mere fact that he attempted would secure him a place in St. Cortez history.

The decision was made. He faced the possible death and stepped toward the sentry and into the unknown.

In the burdened mind of Constable Truck the sound of the peg leg had suddenly become loud and very hollow and the image of another bubble began to form rapidly. It enveloped him. His head swirled. Millions of naked brown feet cut off at the ankles trampled around and around on the inner sides of the film thin bubble. Running feet belonging to no one in particular, randomly changing the assumed bodies to which they could be attached; feet with elongated toes and nails like blades poking into the walls of the bubble pulling it inward toward him.

Cautiously, Montalgar moved closer leaning to one side to lift the wooden leg an inch above the sidewalk, then pushing it forward in the direction of the sentry before quietly setting it down and balancing on it to bring his single foot forward.

In the tightening dark space of the bubble, Constable Truck was gasping for air. He saw a body begin to form from one of the pairs of trampling feet. First there were ankles then a pair of stained khaki trousers appeared.

The would be revolutionaries on the beach saw Montalgar take the pistol from his pocket; saw him aim it at the Constable Truck's face, then they saw him pause locked in the moment, and balancing his peg leg on the flagstone sidewalk he lifted his good leg to kick the automatic rifle away from Constable Truck's side.

In Constable Truck's nightmare bubble the vaporous body

formed. It was tall, slim and muscular. The face formed. Constable Truck recognized Bernard Montalgar's bold and youthful stare. Then he saw Montalgar waving a bloody machete, rush toward him downward and around on the side of the bubble.

Quickly the Constable lifted the flintlock pistol that had been used to shoot Maurice Bishop. He held the rioter in its shaking gunsight, and knew now the owner of those hollow oncoming footsteps. He fired.

Montalgar realized that Constable Truck was awakening. Now the loud snores were cracked and uneven. He saw the agitated eyelids flicker. Hurriedly Montalgar kicked at the rifle with his good leg and the peg leg skidded on the flagstone. The sidewalk slipped from under him. For a moment he sat on air. Then he fell with a loud painful thud. The pistol escaped his grip and clattered into the dry and shallow gutter that ran alongside the barracks.

In the midst of a bellowing snore, Constable Truck awoke with a start. His face compressed with fear. He threw both hands in the air. But swiftly and of their own accord his heels clicked together. He came smartly to attention, whipping his hand up to his forehead. The salute was rapid and flawless. Immediately he reported to Montalgar with a loud and frightened voice.

"Yes sir sir. The rioters sir." Staring down at him with frightened red eyes.

Perplexed and angry Montalgar nodded twice to acknowledge the salute. And almost immediately Constable Truck recognized the still bright and bold face of an older Montalgar. Scared, again his eyes rushed about in search of his rifle.

On the beach the four would-be revolutionaries began laughing automatically, loudly. Then realizing that they would be heard, they allowed themselves to be convulsed by fits of stifled laughter.

"What's the matter constable?" asked Montalgar. Truck looked quickly at him and seeing the alarmed and perplexed expression on the face of the prone man he quickly gathered himself from the events of the dream. Then he looked about and around to make sure that he had not been seen. Satisfied that there were no witnesses, he relaxed.

Despite the Constable Truck's red eyes and sleep wrinkled face he assumed a serious, nose flaring, and official expression. He saw the fallen rifle behind him but having been accustomed to the sheer force of authority he ignored it, placed both hands behind his back, interlaced his fingers, and with earnestness began to pace to and fro.

Seeing this, laughter again began to swell in the stomachs of the men on the beach and they bit hard on their lips.

"Montalgar," the policeman said with emphasis, "you have disturbed the peace. There were many people sleeping on this island that you have awoken with the noise of that fall.

"Yes sir, I know. Can you help me up?" Montalgar stretched out his hand.

"No" said the Constable, pacing back and forth. "You still have now goddam respect. You still don't know who you are. You are shit. I shot you once before and yet, look at you again sitting there on your ass. Still no goddamn respect. Do you know that this barrack was built by the Queen of England and has since been inherited. Look at my new boots made in America from Russian leather. This barracks is an outpost of the empire.

"That's not my business you know sir. Help me up nuh?"

"Help you up. Before I help you up I'll put a kick in your ass."

"What's the matter constable sir?" asked Montalgar. "I came to the barracks was to make a report and my leg slipped."

"What report?"

"Well you see sir, every night a crimson blooded dog steals the last pictures of my dream and as my dream end I hear only voices."

"What crap is that Montalgar. Are you trying to laugh at me. Now you are going to apologize to the King, to the Empire. Look toward me and apologize."

Saying this Constable Truck did a smart about face and now he began to march lifting his legs in the straight high style of the nazis. His black flannel pants flapping back and forth in front of Montalgar's face. His arms swinging up and down in front of his chest. "Apologize godammit, what you waiting for?"

"But officer sir, twenty years ago you shot me. You took one of my legs. Now you is treating me like shit because I fall down. What is this sir?"

"As if you are innocent. You were a damn rioter."

"A long time ago sir, for a good reason Constable Truck. Because of those riots you can able to vote."

"Damn good that did," shouted Truck.

"O.K. Constable Truck, alright I shall apologize sir, but to you not to the King or the Empire."

The officer stopped marching now and was again pacing quietly. Bits of fine grit, crisp, crackled under the soles of the new boots. He stopped and eyed Montalgar. "That's right, apologize to me."

Montalgar, who had painfully propped himself up on his elbows said, "Your Right Honorable Constable Truck, I apologize."

"What crap is that Montalgar. Apologize properly. Add to that trice great, Viceroy, Commander, Demi God, et cetera ... et cetera."

Montalgar bowed his head and said, "Oh king of kings. Oh trice great one, Viceroy, Commander, Demi God, I apologize."

Constable Truck stared at Montalgar with an expression of harsh scorn. Bewildered, Montalgar put his hand under his hat and scratched his head. He quickly decided not to address the constable with high titles anymore. Since it seemed that he not only believed it but that it could make him dangerous.

The Constable was saying , "Now crawl over here and kiss my boot." Montalgar eyed Constable Truck with a growing concern. He now began to worry about his safety. Was this man mad?

But Montalgar also felt violated, put down. He looked at the boots and hesitated. Then he reasoned with himself. 'So what? I will kiss the boots. This foolish ass can't gain nothing by it. He will still be stupid. He is a buffoon in boots. How can anyone feel inferior if I kiss the boots of a foolish man. Now I'll prove that he's a dimwit."

"Constable Truck," Montalgar said. "Come, I will kiss your boots but you must bring them closer to me."

Constable Truck stepped closer and placed his right foot in front of Montalgar.

Montalgar bent his head victoriously and kissed the boot. But feel Constable Truck wiping the bottom of the other boot in his hat. The sour smell of dog shit burned his nostrils.

Humiliation and fear boiled in him, filling him with a dense hatred. But he also was experiencing a feeling of hopelessness in his chest. He became concerned that actually he was a coward.

Constable Truck began to march again, slapping leather to stone. "I don't care what you say, something has to be done about that goddamn wooden leg. It is scaring tourists from the beaches. It is making the island appear underdeveloped. It is ..." Immediately Montalgar saw an opportunity to regain some of his lost dignity.

"Constable Truck, you ain't see we already on our way. We making progress man. We there with the developing and developed nations. We now have interrogation rooms and invisible prisons."

"Montalgar, if I didn't know that you couldn't have thought of that yourself I'd have you tortured for treason and shot."

Montalgar felt frustrared, imprisoned in himself, not only was he physically insulted but even his having an opinion was denied. He considered unleashing the brunt of his opinions on the constable. Or trying to hit the constable on the shin with his peg leg, or even reminding him that he was no Viceroy or Demi-God, but when he weighed his intended actions against the prospect of torture and death, he realized with anger and shame that he was willing to be a rodent, a worm, a nothing rather than face cold blooded execution.

Constable Truck feeling securely in charge, began again to pace the flagstones earnestly.   Montalgar waited.   The constable stopped, turned to Montalgar and said.

"Montalgar, something must be done about the noise of that leg." He paused, seemed to think for a moment and said magnaminously, "I know, stand guard Montalgar, I'll be right back."

"But your mightiness, help me up. Give me a hand nuh."

"No, not yet Montalgar, stand guard. The constable accustomed as chief to the force of sheer authority forgot the rifle as he turned and entered the barracks.

Montalgar eyed the area where his pistol had fallen into the gutter, then eyed the sentry's automatic rifle. He thought for amoment. Then began to drag his body toward the pistol.

His comrades on the beach looked on. They knew that for tonight fate was not on their side. It was over and they had already thought of a few jokes to laugh at over a bottle of rum while they planned the next attack. They saw Montalgar's movements and assumed that he was crawling toward a wall of the barracks to steady himself so as to stand up. They did not know the anger that boiled Montalgar's heart. He was so intent on reaching the pistol that he did not hear the approaching sound of the constable's boots. He was about to stretch out his arm to feel for the pistol when Constable Truck stepped over him and placed himself between Montalgar and the gutter saying, "Montalgar, no need to escape. I have the solution."

Standing between Montalgar and the pistol he stretched out his hand to help Montalgar to his feet. Montalgar examined the officer's outstretched hand, sighed, shook his head and was about to grasp it when Truck pulled his hand back and said, "Wait first, I have to put a kick in your ass."

Montalgar was again perplexed. "Why sir?"

"Man, shut up, turn around."

"But, but sir, but Viceroy, I ... "

"I said shut up." Montalgar heard the shout, saw a flash of polished black. Instinctively he tried to move, but heard the thud and felt the sharp pain rip through his ribs.

Constable Truck stretched down his hand once more. "Now take my hand."

'The bastard,' Montalgar cursed silently. His face twisted with pain. He grasped Constable Truck's hand. The officer pulled him up. Once more he was standing on one foot and a peg leg. His ribs were singing with pain. He straightened his hat and saw the dark outline of the pistol in the gutter. He wanted to shoot holes into Truck, that black police tunic, that arrogant and self-assured black tunic. But realized then that now standing on his wooden leg, he could not bend to pick up his pistol quickly enough without risking falling on his face and revealing the presence of the pistol.

His attention turned to Constable Truck who was holding out a bundle of flags toward him and saying, "This old barracks is filled with flags. Every time the government changes we have a different flag. I also have political prisoners from the first revolution. Now Montalgar, take the flags and tie them to the bottom of the peg leg; that will stop the goddamn noise." Montalgar smiled. The constable saluted. "God bless counter-revolutions."

"Yes and crimson blooded men."

Footnote: The Prime Minister when interviewed by his biographer years later, was asked why he chose the term 'crimson blood' to describe the predators. He replied that he had heeded Camus' warning about kafka's dog. That He wanted to accuse 'people with shadows' but because of Jungian mysticism and Dracula movies he thought the people would interpret the threat as purely psycholoanalytic and would be on the look out for vampires. Therefore he placed many terms in a hat, closed his eyes, and chose one.

GOODBYE GOOD LUCK

Clive had seen that look on his mother's face before, three months ago when his father said, "Beryl I've got good news and I've got bad news." Clive was sitting in the back seat of his father's car. His father was driving him to school. It was early morning and the sunlight made the trees look purple blue at the top of the Blue Mountains.

"Tell me the good news first," his mother said.

"I got the letter from the US immigration. It looks like we will get the visa."

"Now tell me the good news," his mother said. She looked at his father.

"That was the good news."

"You joking. I don't want to migrate to New York City. It good for a vacation, but not to live, not to raise two children."

"Well hear the bad news then," his father said.

Clive listened. His father was quiet. The car sped along.

"My job is moving to another country," his father said.

"CBM is moving?"

"Yes to some place where the labour is cheaper and there are no unions."

Clive didn't want to move to New York either. He was ten. He had heard stories about New York that scared him. Besides he would miss his friends. His sister was seven. Her name was Jasmine and when he told her she was excited. "Aunt Norma lives in America and the clothes she send in the barrell smell nice."

It was raining the October morning when they drove to the American embassy. The air smelled damp. Clive looked at the raindrops on the window. The rain filled the gutters and the gutters overflowed leaving a layer of mud at the side of the street. Clive's mother had dressed him in a white shirt, a tie and blue pants. His father was dressed in his suit and they looked as though they were going to church.

At the embassy the immigration officer who interviewed his father and mother had a yellow mustache. Clive kept looking at the mustache. The mustache looked like the handle bars of his bike. After the interview, the American asked them to hold up their right hand to take the oath.

Clive watched his mustache move up and down. Clive repeated what the American said and his father and mother and sister repeated too.

The blond man stamped visas in the blue passports. They had resident visas. This allowed them to live and work in the USA, Clive's father said to his mother as they drove home. Clive's mother looked out of the side window. She didn't say anything. It was drizzling and the road was wet.

"Other people only have visas that let them visit the USA but not to live there and work, and some applied for student visas that let them go to school but not work. We are lucky Auntie Norma sponsored us. Do you know illegal aliens have to cross over the Mexican and Canadian border in the night ..." His mother remained silent. Clive saw the big truck rushing toward them on the other side of the street. The truck was red. " ... and worse," his father was saying. "Some Haitians try to get to America in small boats and many of them drown in the ...."

Clive saw the truck skid and spin on the wet street. His mother's mouth opened. He heard the brakes, a blur. Their car slammed into the truck.

Every day Clive remembered how still his father was after

the crash, how his face rested in the steering wheel. Now his father just lay there in a coma in the hospital bed in Kingston. Clive heard his mother say to Aunt Norma on the phone that the doctor said he could be in the coma for a week, a month, a year. He just couldn't tell her. His mother started crying and Clive ran outside and climbed the mango tree behind the house.

A month later they were packing suitcases. His mother said she could get a job in America that would make it easier to pay the hospital bills and the mortgage on the house.

Clive wanted to pack everything in his suitcase. He wanted to take the hospital with him and he wanted to pack his dog Rover but Rover wouldn't lie down in the suitcase. He kept jumping out before Clive could zip it up.

"Anyway you can't carry dogs and trees to America," his mother said. "Unless you have special papers."

Clive remembered his father as he looked out the round window of the plane. His sister sat next to him. His mother sat in the seat across the narrow aisle. There had been a lot of people in the airport and a lot of suitcases. There were a lot of people on the plane.

Around him now was the blue sky. His sister looked out of the round window.

"Look Clive I can see the sea down there.

"No Jasmine it's the sky."

"I can see the waves."

"Those are clouds," Clive said.

"Mommy is that the sky or the sea down there?" Jasmine said.

Her mommy did not hear her. She was looking at the backs of heads of the people seated in the plane in front of her and not seeing them. Her face was silent. Clive had seen his mother's face like that before. Jasmine repeated the question.

THE DEATH & BIRTH OF CONRAD GRAHAM

Conrad Graham, a tall, slender eater of English apples, had since the end of August noticed a stirring in his stomach. It was not at all painful nor totally uncomfortable. It merely felt as if something was slowly, silently, discreetly, making a life for itself in his stomach.

He first realized that maybe he would have to accomodate a new change in his body as he was sitting with his mother in the center of a sunny Sunday afternoon looking out from the verandah at the aquamarine sea. Because it was Sunday and sunny and his mother was sitting next to him dressed in flowered print, he concluded that he was merely having a slight attack of gas.

He described the sensations to his mother who sat opposite

him on the verandah of the stately manor house built of walaba wood by his dead father. His mother, plump, preoccupied and reading Agatha Christie, her back to the white sun, lifted her round face and looked at him with large attentive black eyes over wire-rimmed glasses.

"Go and see Dr. McMillan," she said.

"Why? He will only tell me I have worms."

"Maybe you do," his mother mumbled, sinking back into the depths of mystery.

"With doctors you need luck," Conrad insisted. "They tell you what's wrong and then experiment on you until you die."

His mother didn't look up.

"Only the lucky survive," he continued, "and in August I don't feel very lucky."

"The butler did it," his mother said emphatically.

Conrad did not go to the doctor. For the next week he concentrated on his work and after that he hung around with his friends at 'Beach Bums' and argued concretely about theoretical assumptions convinced that if he ignored whatever it was and continued a regular routine the problem with his stomach would go away.

By the end of the week curiosity got the better of him. As he sat at his desk working, he probed his stomach with his forefinger and thought that he had discovered a lump from which he could trace threadlike tentacles branching toward his legs and upward to his worried self-awareness.

And then he was forced to convince himself that he was no expert on how his stomach felt, for he had never probed it that way before and so he had no way of knowing.

The next Sunday morning, as usual, he played the organ in Lordstown's Lady of the Sacrament Church inspiring the voices of the choir and congregation, but, in the middle of the final hymn of the morning mass, the old priest Father Placid heard a flurry of organ keys and pedals. He turned and saw Conrad throw his head back and his eyes followed Conrad as he lifted from the organ stool and soared plaintively above and beyond the angels painted on the roof of the church and into a sad blue sky. The sudden improviso took the singers by surprise, disarranged their voices and eventually left them hymnless.

As Conrad soared the churchgoers eyes followed him. Father Placid coughed loudly and Conrad discovered himself alone in the sad blue sky beyond everything and anyone without the support of the voices of the choir. So, rapidly, in a thunder of chords, he came crashing back through the roof and into the congregation and onto the stool. Then he paused, buttoned his jacket, rearranged himself, and struck the initial chords again. Cautiously the choir joined in and then the congregation followed.

After the mass had ended he stood waiting in the inner courtyard outside the vestry beside the fishpond for Father Placid, probing his stomach with his forefinger, trying to decipher for certain if something in fact was growing there.

The faithful slowly left the comforting sanctuary of the church and Father Placid, tall in his white robes with chiseled wrinkles like waves over his forehead, came hurrying through the courtyard. He saw Conrad standing at the fishpond and smiled mischievously.

"Not smoking any little cigarettes, are we?" he said hurrying past Conrad.

"No Father," Conrad answered hurrying after him and unbuttoning his jacket with its white shirt and dark tie. "I went ahead of myself today ... unconsciously."

Father Placid smiled but did not answer and continued hurrying toward the vestry.

"Father, I must confess."

"Too late. The confession box is closed for the day. Come back tomorrow between three and four."

"That's not the problem, Father ..."

Father Placid reached the door of the vestry and stopped.

Turning the doorknob he said to Conrad, "Son, there are three things that rule man. God, the bowels and the bladder."

"Well you see Father, the problem is ..."

"Talk quickly son, I have to pee."

"Well Father ... I have nothing to confess."

Rubbing his palms together, Father Placid said, "If you read the Bible you will find you have a lot to confess. Goodbye, son."

Father Placid rushed through the doorway of the vestry and for the rest of that Sunday and the next Conrad read the Bible, taking it with him to the faded government office where he culled the previous year's statistics from racks of pink import and blue export receipts bound with string and brown paper.

As he read the Bible, he probed his stomach. That afternoon, he knelt in the confession box. There in the enclosed semi-darkness with purity of the priest on the other side of the partition like his alter ego, like the purer part of himself that he was appealing to to free him of his fears, he confessed and felt at one with the holiness of the priest as agent of the singular benevolent God, undisturbed by the certainty of Father Placid's incessant yawning on the other side of the mahogony of sins. In response to his confession,

Father Placid awarded him a penance of three Hail Mary's.

Each night he read the twenty-third psalm and promised God that if he was cured he would not sin again, not in the slightest or for the rest of his life. The next two weeks he divided his time between prayer, the confession box and the solitary wonder of the outhouse.

There amid the dull smell of night earth and the lingering scent of brown frogs he tried to force out whatever was there in his stomach while he stared at the unpainted, weather-washed door and contemplated the dark insides of his bowels and the endless and silent hole below the seat. His visits to the confession box became so frequent that by the end of August he had solemnly emptied himself of his sins and the silent discomfort in his stomach ceased.

Then, like a blow to his faith, it was confirmed for him that something was actually wrong.

On the last despondent Saturday afternoon in August, sure now that everything was alright, he fornicated with Sola, the servant girl. As they made love shrouded in urgent whispers to avoid his mother's marvelous ears and her telling him that he was disrespecting the crucifix above his bedhead, Sola looked up at him with her bold sleepy eyes and whispered, "What's in your stomach?"

The whisper momentarily reduced the urgency of their efforts and as they were done and Sola was slipping her short and heavily rounded body into her glistening black slip of fake silk, he looked at her and discovered the world had become somewhat distant and intangible.

Over the next two days, the constant probing of his stomach allowed him to calculate that whatever it was, actually Jesus Christ, growing in his stomach, grew at a rate of a millimeter a day.

On Wednesday of the second week in September the sky was sullen with the expectation of a predicted hurricane. He stopped working and looked out the cloudy window panes through quiet eyes in a brown, round and pensive face at the pious grey sky over the island.

He imagined a list of people who better deserved this wicked fate. He started from Gattie the Indian who seemed preserved in alcohol and proceeded to all the sick members of death squads and right then the thought struck him that maybe he was no better than them, maybe he had done some terrible thing. He began again searching his memory for sins he had not yet confessed to the priest. And so he remembered that day as a boy when he stole a half-a-penny from his older brother's pocket. "But that was nothing," he thought and became scared that the fact might be that he had emptied himself of his confessions and the thing was still growing in his stomach. He then considered inventing sins that would justify its presence. Then it struck him that, after all, stealing the penny may have been a big sin for he had lied, he had said it wasn't him and maybe that had caused his brother to become a liar too, and maybe that was why his brother embezzled money at the bank and had to flee the country.

He stared at the sky. It was void of anything but his fears and his sadness and Conrad became convinced that the stealing of the penny was a mortal sin.

He left the office and headed for the church. The rain was drizzling on his head making his white shirt wet and transparent on his skin as he hurried to the confession box, his hands pushed in his pocket, his head hung forward, eyes staring at the wet cobblestone street, elated that at last maybe he had found a solution.

It was half an hour before the priest was due to come down to relieve the sinners of the weight of their guilt. Conrad pulled back the heavy maroon velvet curtain that covered the back of the confession booth, entered, pulled it close behind him, knelt and waited in the darkness of the confession box which felt as personal as a coffin.

In the silent aura of the church, his mind settled and drifted off to delve into the deep waters of sleep from which he had been barred by nights of worry. Half an hour later he was abruptly awakened by Father Placid singing a popular calypso.

> *"You making yourself a puppet show, Melda*
> *You making yourself a bloody clown*
> *Running 'round the country looking for obeah*
> *And your perspiration smell so strong ...*
> *Ah still ain't go marry to you."*

Conrad cleared his throat and abruptly the priest stopped. "Bless you for you have sinned."

Conrad began his lengthy confession about stealing the penny, desperately analyzing all the possible permutations of that single wicked act, and carried it logically to the point where that insignificant act resulted in degrading the morality of his older brother and beyond that.

He could again hear Father Placid's deep yawns. Then in the middle of his confession the priest began to cough .

Then there was a heavy silence as if Father Placid was no longer in the other side of the confession box. He was wondering whether the priest had fallen asleep, when a loud swish of the curtain sounded behind him. He turned. Father

Placid was standing there looking firmly at him. "Out you go. It is a bad day for weak confessions. The sky is overcast."

Slowly Conrad stood up, bent his head and walked toward the door. Father Placid felt his sadness and called him back.

"Conrad, wait. I haven't prescribed your penance yet. What is you favorite fruit?"

Conrad felt his stomach. "I like English apples."

"Apples!" the priest exclaimed, quickly making the sign of the cross over his chest and face.

"They are sinful fruit. Since before Adam they have always been forbidden, but no-one ever listened."

Conrad saw the wrinkled seriousness of the priest's aging face and again the distance of the world asserted itself.

"For your penance stop eating English apples and don't forget to say your prayers."

Conrad thanked him, said goodbye and walked toward the door under the high, silent, arched gothic roof with its silent painted angels and the pious ceramic saints praying in the cubicles along the wall. He felt close to these silent figures and as he approached the street he saw the church door again as if for the first time with its heavy iron hinges, its tall arched presence, the seams and cracks in the heavy wood. High above it a sad stained-glass Jesus clothed only in a diaper with arms stretched out and bleeding palms nailed to the cross. In the middle of his chest, a bleeding apple was wrapped in tight thorns.

Conrad walked under the nail wounds in the feet of Jesus. A drop of blood fell into the container of holy water at the door. He dipped his finger into the quiet reddened water, made the sign of the cross over his chest and face, then gave in to his mother's advice and headed for the doctor.

The doctor lived on the other end of the town where the large white two-storied houses with tall arched galleries had been built by the retired pirates and slave owners but were now inhabited largely by politicians.

After he had knocked twice, a middle-aged nurse opened the door. "Young man, you can catch a cold like that."

Only then did he realize that the rain had plastered the shirt to his skin.

"Come in," the nurse said, holding the door open and scolding him with her eyes. He wiped his feet on the mat of coconut fibres. She walked ahead leading him into the inner depths of the house toward the waiting room. His footsteps sounded loud in the clean hallway with its faded bare white walls. There was no-one else in the waiting room. It was barely furnished. Conrad sat and waited in the clean worn silence of the room. After about five minutes, the stooping shoulders and long faced white head of Dr. McMillan looked at him from the door through wire spectacles.

Conrad stood up, "Good afternoon, Doctor."

"Hello, Conrad. Come with me. How is your mother?"

They walked into his office.

Conrad took off his shirt while staring at the wall and faded diploma from the University of Edinburgh next to shelves filled with dusty medical journals.

"Oh, she's fine."

"Still reading Agatha Christie?" Dr. McMillan rested his stethoscope on Conrad's chest.

"Yes."

The doctor walked around him and put the stethoscope on his back and listened.

"I think you have worms," he said, removing the stethoscope from his ears.

"Doctor, there is something growing in my stomach. I can feel it right here."

The doctor pressed his hand on Conrad's stomach. Conrad held his frail hand and guided his hand to the lump. Dr. McMillan nodded, walked over to his cluttered desk and found a rubber hammer. He walked back to Conrad and struck his knee. The leg kicked. "You have a bad case of Mexican worms. You not only need worm medicine but a strong dose of salts to purge your bowels."

The doctor wrote the prescription and handed it to him.

"Take this Saturday night and on Sunday morning stay near to the outhouse. It will make your bowels growl like thunder."

Conrad was warmed by the good news. He said goodbye to the doctor and was leaving the office when he forced himself to say, "Doctor, I think the problem is worse than that, Doctor."

The old doctor shrugged helplessly, calling up the sadness of a lifetime into his eyes.

"Maybe, but take the medicine anyway and come back and see me by next week." Conrad sagged inside and left with a lukewarm hope.

On that Saturday morning under the impatient eyes of his mother, Conrad examined the label of the bottle of medicine, trying to determine whether the pharmacist had correctly deciphered the doctor's writing. Conrad concluded he had since the pharmacist writing was as bad as the doctor's and he didn't understand either.

Slowly he lifted his head back, squeezed his nostrils shut, put the bottle to his lips and carried out the ill-tasting act of faith.

That evening his throat was defiant. At the taste of the epsom salts, it sealed itself shut. He grimaced, spluttered, choked, spat, and groaned before he could empty the glass.

That night he slept well.

The next morning he awoke to the quivering expectation of his buttocks and full, distended stomach bubbling with a heavy liquid.

Immediately he rushed to the outhouse and released the first barrage. It spewed out with the tonal variety of a battlefield.

Despite the activity, the outhouse stood as austere as a British butler as if innocent and unaware of the man inside. The forceful contractions of Conrad's stomach sucked the rest of his body toward it. The tangy, sour, muscular effort of its contracting was upsetting the silent effort of whatever it was that was growing there.

He felt a gentle tickling sensation all over his body as if millions of treads were moving about under his skin. The tickling spread about the muscles and bones of his chest and in the minute crevices of spinal vertebrae and the large bones of his thighs and hips. Conrad became amazed, then afraid.

His heart began a wild race. Drops of cold nauseous sweat appeared on his forehead. Again his stomach contracted and relaxed. Unable now to control or resist the tickling, Conrad began to chuckle and then to laugh uncontrollably amid a barrage of loud farts.

His mother rushed to the outhouse and banged on the door.

"Conrad, open up. Open the door this minute."

Conrad unlatched the door. His mother examined him with a look of outraged amazement, sitting there chuckling and sweating with his bony knees and his pants around his ankles.

"Is everything alright?" she asked.

He looked at her, pleading with a pained look in his eyes, and tried to describe what was happening, but his stomach contracted again and he was caught in a fit of laughter. His mother, confused by his pain and his laughter, said, "Have you gone mad, Conrad? Stop it. Stop it. Let me warn you, this is what happens when you keep a crucifix over the bed you carouse in."

When he got out of the outhouse, his mother was waiting at the dining room table with a hot cup of tea. He drank it and rushed to the outhouse again. By mid-day, his stomach was resting. That night his sleep was smug and vacant and the next morning he woke hazy and pleasant after a dream of floating in a translucent field of green grass and yellow flowers. It was already eight o'clock and he hurried to the shower with its cold concrete floor.

He was soaping his chest with the white lather of green Palmolive soap when he noticed that his thighs were heavy with the growth of thick white hairs.

Immediately he began soaping his thighs, rubbing them hard, and the white hairs began breaking off and swirling with the soapy water through the drain in the floor and he noticed that where the white hairs broke off, the skin of his thighs itched and burned as if he had bruised it.

Scared, he quickly stepped out of the shower and gently dried and examined the minute white dots where the new hairs had broken off. He felt the strange new hairs, rubbing them between his thumb and forefinger. There was a coarse, thick quality to them.

Conrad entered the dazed space of being in a situation where he knew something dreadful was happening to him, something he couldn't shrug away, or ignore, or maybe even do anything about, and something, too, that had made itself inextricably a part of him.

Conrad went to the office with his mind closed fiercely against the experience. But, by mid morning, he was once more in Dr. McMillan's office. This time he had to wait while the doctor attended to an old man and three mothers with screaming babies. When it was his turn, he quickly dropped his pants and showed the new white hairs to Dr. McMillan.

Dr. McMillan asked him to remove his shirt and listened to his back with the stethoscope.

"Now, open your buccal cavity."

"Where's that?"

"Your mouth, son."

Conrad opened his mouth. The doctor shone a small light in it.

"Well, it doesn't look like worms and I don't know what to say. But I must add that you skin is taking on a greenish-gray pallor."

"Can you recommend anything? Anything?"

"No son. Sooner or later, doctors realize that all their lives they have been priests. Priests recommend prayer. We recommend laxatives. Same thing. We console the dying with lies, just like priests. We tell them they are not really dying, the priest tells them about life after death."

That night Conrad's mother examined the threadlike hairs protruding from her son's legs. She said, "Come, let me shave them."

"No, no. They burn and itch like my own skin when they break."

His mother sighed, muttered a prayer, thought for a moment, "Come with me."

She led him to the bathroom and filled the bathtub with a mixture of hot water, bleach and detergent.

"Now, soak in it as hot as you can bear it."

The next morning his mother came to his room to look at his thighs. He saw her enter through the door but somehow his mind did not register that she was distinct from the walls at which he was staring. Not until she spoke.

The hard white hairs that had been in the mixture shriveled up, which his mother thought was a good sign, except that overnight the hairs had grown longer and thicker. His mother, sitting on the bed next to him, noticed the green and gray pallor of his skin. But she was silent about it until he told her about the growing tender bump in his head that he had to comb around every morning.

"Its gets bigger everyday." he said.

"And Dr. McMillan said it was the first time in his thirty-one years of practice he ever met a case like yours. Don't you see? This is somebody's dirty hand on you. Conrad, I think you better go and see Papa Osaitin," his mother said.

"Who? The obeah man?"

"There are things in heaven and earth not dreamt of by philosophers."

"Sounds like a quote from Agatha Christie," he said sadly.

"You joking Conrad. I don't believe in obeah myself. But this looks like a case for Papa Osaitin."

"Are you going to work, Mother?"

As he got dressed, his slacks fitted too close for the heavy growth of white hairs were bulky under his slacks. Driving to work that morning he again noticed the lack of distinction between objects or rather that it was as if everything was subject to an aura that robbed the individual objects of the distinction that held them within a rigid structure.

He had stopped at a cross street so that a group of blue-uniformed Anglican School girls could pass. The two-story buildings of limestone and shingles, the overhanging galleries with the family life on the second floor and the bolts of cloth and other merchandise on sale on the first seemed meaningless, as if abandoned, and the black narrow street appeared to lead nowhere. After the schoolgirls had crossed the road, he did not realize that they had or that the car was not moving or that there were impatient motorists behind him, until the horns jerked the life and meaning back into the street. Even then he felt as if he should sit there and keep the town in this trancelike state of waiting. He had the sense of a soft clay sculpture gradually hardening.

When he got to the office, his supervisor, an East Indian, was waiting and looking at him with a red stare that had been permanently diffused by alcohol.

"Hi, Conrad. I need to know how much banana boxes we imported last year.

"Hold on," Conrad said walking to his desk and bending to pull open the lower drawer.

"What's a leaf doing in your head?"

"What leaf?" Conrad said pulling out a brown hardpaper file.

The supervisor reached, held the leaf and pulled. It didn't budge, but Conrad felt the pull deep inside his head.

"Ouch!" The supervisor quickly withdrew his trembling hand.

"It's tangled in your hair, man."

Impatiently Conrad discussed the figures. He wanted to put his hand into his hair. He wanted the supervisor to leave.

He wanted to feel the leaf and dismiss the absurdity of his fears. The supervisor's breath smelled of rum and mint candy.

Eventually the supervisor left the office. Immediately Conrad put his hand in his hair and searched for the leaf. He found it and pulled gently. It felt solidly grounded to something that extended from inside his skull. He felt along it and found a small branch. He pulled at it. Inside his skull there was a tickling and painful sensation and he felt himself getting a headache. He jumped up and headed straight for Dr. McMillan's office.

"Well, it seems there is a tree growing inside. With that diagnosis, I can prescribe some weed killer," Dr. McMillan said sitting across the desk from Conrad.

"That's not a good idea, Doc," Conrad said noticing how easily he was getting angry. "If the plant dies inside me what will happen to the branches and the roots? I mean, how are you going to pull it from my brain and what of the hole left in my skull if you do?"

"O.K., son. No need to be rude. What kind of seeds have you been eating?"

"English apples."

"Well, no need to worry. English apple trees don't grow in the tropics."

Conrad was exasperated. Dr. McMillan say the incredulous and angry expression on his face.

"Look, don't take it out on me. I know your mother and I knew your father so I am tolerating you. Your father was a good representative of the Crown."

Conrad listened as the doctor changed the subject. "We now have a bunch of rabble-rousing, inept ..." He realized that the doctor was an old man lost in another time.

" ... bribe-taking politicians." That he really wanted to help but couldn't and Conrad let him change the subject.

" ... take even the chairs in your dining-room. Your father had them built straight-backed so that people would sit properly when they ate and the passages in the house they are narrow so that you have to walk erect and in a single-file."

"And the first governor of Jamaica was a pirate, a damn thief."

Dr. McMillan looked at Conrad quietly, not quite understanding the relevance of the comment, but he was willing to allow Conrad any small victories. Dr. McMillan shrugged. These days he dreamt of himself in women's clothing visiting gravesites and he preferred memories to argument and contradictions that could go on forever. He shrugged again. "What can I tell you Fidel. Wait here a moment."

The doctor left the office. Conrad waited and was considering the ridiculous nature of his predicament when Dr. McMillan came back leafing through the Encyclopaedia of Plants.

"Confirmed. From the leaves I can tell, it's an English apple tree."

The next day Conrad went to work wearing a hat. He noticed that the roots growing from his legs became agitated and tickled when he walked past the field next to the parking lot which was plowed for agricultural experiments.

That afternoon Conrad drove into the countryside to see Papa Osaitin. He parked the car at the bottom of Jack Fruit Hill, got out and looked up. At the top of the hill he saw the red flag flying on the tall bamboo pole that Sola had told him to look for, but he saw no road leading to it, not even a dirt path.

He closed the car door, made sure he had the fee in his pocket, then pushed through heavy, matted bush marked by the paths of imaginary snakes, large green lizards, thick with insects that stung the back of his neck and arms.

The white roots growing from his legs became agitated with a desire to enter the soil. Determinedly, he made his way upwards in the direction of the red flag he could no longer see.

Eventually he pushed his way into a clearing and immediately bent to scratch his legs. When Conrad looked up, he saw a man with his back turned sitting on a stool in front of a small house of rain-blackened wood. The front door was a geometry of colors. He noticed also that behind the man was an old large copper basin that was used long ago to boil molasses. He stepped forward toward the man.

"That 'nuf now. Stop right there and state your case," Papa Osaitin said, his back turned to Conrad.

The heavy voice seemed to come from the back of Osaitin's head. Conrad had the impression of looking at a mouthless face covered with graying hair.

"Papa Osaitin, an apple tree is growing in my stomach."

There was a short silence then the deep bass of the obeah man's voice sounded.

"Well, well. You know once I was respected man. Now people only come to me when they have impossibles and absurdities. I bet you went to the doctor already and he said he can't do nothing."

"Yes."

"I bet you went to the priest and the prayers didn't work."

"Yes."

"Aye, hae! What I tell you. All I get is the rejects. This is disrespect. Once only my presence would heal the sick but now ... Well, anyway take one hundred dollars from your pocket and put it in the copper."

Conrad did as he was told.

"O.K. Now here is what you will do. Drink a glassful of your first pee in the morning mixed with aloes and sea water."

The thought of the mixture made Conrad's throat tighten. Looking at the back of Papa Osaitin head, Conrad asked, "Will it work?"

"Well, there is a cure for everything but is to find it, and it is always the medicine you didn't take that didn't cure you. I like it when intelligent people come to me because even when I cure them they never be sure I did it, for if the medicine does work they give me no credit. They go back to their known world by saying I, Papa Osaitin, had nothing to do with it. Yet, it don't matter, you have no choice. Drink it. Take your medicine and when you pee a second time, throw it over your shoulder."

Conrad did not, could not accept the advice of the obeah man and as the week passed the roots thickened and became increasingly agitated and one night after passing through the narrow passageways of his father's house and eating supper at the dining table, he got into his car and drove to Lordtown's Square where there is a grassy circle and a statue of the unreturned soldiers. He walked through the moist grass to the left of the right of the statue and removed his pants. The roots began to grow toward the soil. Townspeople passed by hardly noticing him.

But Sola was walking along Halifax Street and saw him, and ran toward him embracing him. The roots entered through her flesh, and the buildings of the town became as malleable as soft putty. She blended with him. Their bodies became the single trunk of a tree. The branches sprouted from the trunk. As the soft cement of the streets and houses dried, their consciousness widened until they were no more and the inhabitants of Lordtown began to walk in straight lines and sit in straight-backed chairs for cups of tea.

Years later, the faithful discovered red sap in the trunk and would stab it on Good Friday to prove it was on that day Jesus ascended into heaven and the Queen's birthday parade would climax in front of the tree and children would play under it and birds would nest in it.

And years later, Malcolm Brown, the unsuccessful revolutionary, would try to chop it down.

ABOUT A MANNER OF DRESS

The conversation occured on a hot night in August. I will not disclose the identity of the speakers, nor mine for that matter, nor their occupation, nor height, manner of dress.

I will say only that the conversation occured two days after the warm blood of a man flowed smoothly and continuously from a sliced artery in his neck.

I will not disclose the man's color since it is felt that it is natural for men of certain colors and nationalities to die in a certain manner. That a Japanese spewed out his stomach with a ritual dagger is worth but a yawn. Only a shrug is appropriate to the news that the corpse of a man with a vowel ending his last name was found stuffed in the trunk of a dusty Oldsmobile with two bullets shot in the back of his head, while according to forensic experts, he was kneeling, head bent forward, hands tied behind his back.

These men were not animals. When their obituaries are read, the words loyal, dedicated, brave will be heard among the flowers.

Such were the nature of my thoughts when I overheard the conversation of two men on a train traveling north to the suburbs of a certain city. It is the nature of man to act normal in absurd situations, so I listened.

" ... They are animals. What do you expect? What else but an animal will drive a car that could break down in a neighborhood of decent people."

" ... Killed?"

"But of course we killed them. They are animals."

Who are the speakers? Should I disclose the century, the hour, their dress, the continent? No!

Not knowing she was to be evicted, an overweight grandmother hears her door crash open, sees men enter. They are armed. Shotguns. Revolvers. She takes up her kitchen knife. A shotgun blast echoes. The hand holding the knife is blown off at the wrist. She clutches the bloody stump. The shotgun echoes again. The wind rushes into her chest through the hole torn open by the lead.

" ... Why shoot her again?"

" ... is an animal."

"She is ...?"

I will not disclose the color of the woman lying dead in the hallway of her apartment.

I will disclose the species of the dog. It was a bull terrier. Its mouth filled with a baby's head. The distraught father called the authorities, the same type that went to the grandmother.

They came with a tranquilizer gun, spoke quietly, sedated the dog, removed the baby's head and drove the dog to the City Pound.

"Why not shoot the dog?"

"The dog is a pet."

That's all I shall say about that time, that manner of dress.

E. B. Baisden on The Death and Birth of Conrad Graham

This tale owes its existence to the juxtaposition of a dying
John Oliver Killens and an assignment to teach about plants.
I met John O. Killens three months before I was saddened by
the rumour that he dying of stomach cancer.
On a September morning when he was in the hospital and I
stood in the science room at PS 138 leafing through a textbook
on plants, I sat down and wrote:
"Conrad Graham had noticed a stirring in his stomach."
After adjustments, it read:

> "Conrad Graham, a tall, slender eater of English apples,
> had since the end of August noticed a stirring in his
> stomach. It was not at all painful nor totally
> uncomfortable. It merely felt as if something was slowly,
> silently, discreetly, making a life for itself in his stomach."

On "The Death and Birth of Conrad Graham"

Like men, cultures realizing that they are threatened by disruptive changes, have two choices, they can marshall their defenses by calling on their gods, including the flag, the beauty of the country and its people, a sense of guilt and betrayal, or they can go to war.

The individual within the culture threatened by an ailment that could lead to impending death is also given two similar choices, he / she can appeal to his gods or he can go to the doctor.

What today constitutes Caribbean was produced by an effort of the African people and native Caribbeans calling on the gods and going to war to rid themselves of the European ailment, and the effort of the European ailment to survive, to impose itself, calling on the same two forces - preachers and guns.

Of the many combinations of these two choices, Conrad Graham first chooses to go to the priest only to find that his god is unreachable.

What does a man do in this situation? Think of the African on the Caribbean plantation, the Jew in the concentration camp, Che Guevara at the moment of his death, his gun beyond his grasp.

Man must then do things for himself. He must now use temporal means. He must go to war.

Thus Conrad Graham goes to the doctor, and only after, to the

207

obeah man.

The cure offered by the obeah man, doctor of the natives, is obviously irrational. But the irrational exists at the very basis of culture. It is what maintains the institutions of culture.

The basis of Christianity, Islam, etc. is that life exists after death. Capitalism is based on an addiction, derived from the irrational assumption that well being can be purchased. Socialism was an irrational effort to create a spiritual man through material means. That one and one is equal two is also an irrational assumption, as is love, which is the basis of some relationships. But such is the task of man. He must define himself and his world. So what does Conrad Graham do? Does he drink his pee mixed with aloes and sea water and thus re-establish himself in the irrational essence of the culture?